# MURDER IS
# A GAMBLE

*by*

GLENN M. BARNS

COMPLETE AND UNABRIDGED

LAWRENCE E. SPIVAK

*Publisher*

A BESTSELLER MYSTERY, NO. 162

*Bestseller Mysteries, Mercury Mysteries, and Jonathan Press Mysteries are published under the* MERCURY IMPRINT

MERCURY PUBLICATIONS, INC., 570 Lexington Ave., New York 22, N. Y.

# CHAPTER ONE

"Keep a sharp eye on him," the chief had said, "and a nose, too, for that matter. There is a smell about him and his proposition that I don't quite like."

Still, the fat retainer had sufficiently dulled the chief's sense of smell, and there I was, two weeks and three thousand miles later, not much wiser than I had been at the start.

Not that I was dissatisfied. I was in a hotel which was a lot better than I would have paid for with my own money, eating in better restaurants, smoking better cigars. And to date I had not been called on to do a tap of work. It was too good to be true, or even honest.

I lay there on one of the very comfortable twin beds, watching the Colonel struggle with his collar button. Even doing that, he contrived to look dignified, slightly pompous, unbelievably self-assured. The collar finally anchored, he reached for his dress tie. That was entirely beyond him, as we both knew perfectly well, but I watched him fumble with it for a time.

"Come on over," I said eventually. "I'll fix it for you."

Surprise and gratification were nicely blended, exactly as always, on the beefy, brick-red face he turned toward me. "Why, Jonathan, that is kind of you. My fingers are a bit stiff this evening." It would have choked the old fraud to admit that he didn't know how to tie a bow tie properly. His voice was deep, low, as dramatic as an amateur performance of *East Lynne*. As he bent over the bed I noticed that the point of one side of the cherished waxed mustache was beginning to droop slightly.

The tie operation completed, he walked over to the closet to put on his dinner coat. Then he stood before the mirror and carefully adjusted a white linen handkerchief in the left breast pocket.

"Huh-uh," I told him. "It's about six inches too far out. You aren't supposed to be able to blow your nose without taking it out of your pocket."

He tucked the handkerchief in to an acceptable depth without comment. There was no denying that he looked well-groomed and prosperous as the

3

very devil standing there in the new, well-cut dinner coat. The bulging stomach somehow helped rather than hindered the effect. He was a movie director's conception of a retired army officer, and for all I know maybe they actually look like that.

"Better smear a little more wax on that left mustache. It's beginning to sag on you."

He did so, gravely, without protest. "Really, Jonathan, I fail to see how I could get along without you. I scarcely miss not having my man along."

"I'll bet you don't, at that," I agreed. "But I'm more concerned with what you are going to do with me. Just why am I on this excursion, Colonel?"

"My dear boy, I've explained all that to you. I have reason to believe an attempt might be made on my life. I'm somewhat interested in preventing that. If, in spite of all precautions, the attempt should be successful, I am interested in seeing the perpetrator brought to justice. Therefore I applied to your employer and you are the result."

"But what and whom am I guarding you against? Think how much better I could operate if I wasn't entirely in the dark."

"Jonathan, if I wanted to make plain the whole affair I needn't have met the somewhat flattering figure Mr. Watson placed on your services. I wanted a man who could foresee and meet eventualities. I'm satisfied that I have him. Why can't you be satisfied as well? Aren't you comfortable?"

"Yeah, I'm comfortable." I opened a fresh bottle of beer from the supply in the ice bucket beside the bed, and lit my pipe. I knew that the tinge of reproach in the look the Colonel cast at the beer was not because it was charged to him, but because he had a low opinion of beer as a beverage. "I'll just lie here drinking beer until somebody knocks you off; then I'll open that brief case of yours, read the letter you say you have there for me, and try to pin it on the party you name in the letter. I think you're too blamed mysterious, but it's your neck."

The Colonel beamed at me. "That's the spirit, my boy. But you must not think that I distrust you. It is simply that a man of my extensive financial interests unavoidably makes certain enemies, because of matters of such far-reaching importance that it is unwise to discuss them with a soul." That was the way he always talked.

"Okay, Colonel, okay. But just to prove you really are getting a detective for your money, I'll say now that I figure your financial interests extend just as far as that pack of cards on the table, and no farther."

He didn't get sore. "Tut, tut," he said mildly. "Merely the relaxation I indulge in to clear my mind. You over-estimate any slight dexterity I may possess. And now, even considering your appalling habit of dressing in five

minutes, it will be time to dine as soon as you are ready. Will you have a
Scotch and soda with me?"

"No, thanks — I'm a beer man before dinner." I slid out of bed and
started to dress, watching those long, supple fingers mixing a drink. Those
fingers which were too stiff to cope with a bow tie, but which could deal an
ace off the bottom of the deck as neatly as anything I've ever seen.

He turned in time to see me putting on the coat to my brown tweed suit.
He raised his eyebrows in a familiar routine. "Tweeds for dinner, my boy?"
As usual, he managed to put a "that sort of thing would never do with us"
inflection into his voice.

I didn't say anything. No one likes to be called a bum, even by another
bum. He knew as well as I did that I had brought exactly two suits along
on this trip. I took my little 25-calibre Mauser from the table and slid it
into the built-in pocket in the left side of the coat, under the arm. The
loose-hanging fabric hid the shape of the gun entirely, but it rested there
comfortably accessible to one brief motion.

He nodded approval at the gun. "You know your business, Jonathan,
although I trust it won't be needed at dinner. Come, we'll go down."

The tall brunette kid I had noticed on duty when we checked in the
night before was running the elevator again. The Colonel noticed her, too,
and turned on the magnetism. "You look charming tonight, my dear —
utterly charming." He beamed approvingly at her, dropping a hand on her
shoulder with a gesture which might have been a fatherly pat.

The girl wasn't having any. She twisted her shoulder away with a fluid
motion. "Thank you," she said coldly, rather like a Junior Leaguer being
accosted by a tramp. We rode down to the lobby without another word.
As we stepped out of the car, I met her eyes and raised my brows a trifle,
giving her a quick impersonal grin intended to emphasize the fact that
the pass came from the Colonel, not me. She didn't give me a flicker of
acknowledgment.

In the hotel dining room, where he was the only man in dinner clothes,
the Colonel carried on without a break, beaming appreciatively at the waitress
who brought us a menu. She was a somewhat washed-out blonde of uncertain years, although I wasn't uncertain as to the fact that she would never
see thirty again. She was just beginning to approach plumpness, a fact which
her crisp green uniform and uncorseted state did not attempt to hide. Following the Colonel's eyes, I noticed that her legs were fairly commendable.
All in all she struck me as a far more suitable object of his attentions than
the kid in the elevator.

She met his appraising look with a pleasant smile, generously including
me. "Evening, gentlemen."

The Colonel took the menu and studied it thoughtfully, letting other considerations slide for the moment. He allowed few things to interfere with the serious business of food. He gave his order carefully, with elaborate instructions as to the preparation of the steak and the salad. She wrote down the order but appeared to be ignoring the instructions. When he finished, I said I would have the same. You seldom went wrong duplicating the Colonel's order.

"Young lady," he said, actually giving his mustache a twirl, "we are in the unfortunate position of being strangers in your city. What can you suggest in the way of entertainment here?"

She appeared to give it some reflection. "Gee, sir, this is a pretty lively town. Lots of good night spots around."

"Ah, that sounds encouraging. It is music, laughter, bright lights which we seek. But there is a difficulty. Nothing is so dull as gaiety without feminine companionship. Yet we are strangers in the city."

They reminded me of a couple of well-rehearsed wrestlers going through all of the necessary motions before winding it up.

"You can meet lots of nice girls anxious to go places around here. A couple of gents like you fellows won't have any trouble."

"Would it be too much to hope that you might do us the honor? Now, before you refuse, remember that as a guest of the hotel I have virtually been introduced formally to you."

I found myself getting interested in what her answer to that might be. Her mother's strictness would have been a nice touch.

"Well," she hesitated, "I never go out with strangers. Besides, I'm on duty until ten o'clock."

And so the Colonel made a date with her for ten-fifteen. "Surely you have a friend," he suggested. "My secretary here" — nodding to me — "will be more than happy to accompany us."

She indicated a red-headed girl waiting on the table across the room. Not a bad-looking girl, younger and slimmer than herself. "Vera might go. Would she be okay? She's a swell kid."

"Absolutely," I said, feeling it was time for me to say something. "Vera will be fine." Actually, Vera didn't strike me as too bad under the circumstances.

"Colonel," I said, when we were alone at the table, "this sounds like great stuff, but is it smart? If you're in trouble, you shouldn't be hitting the night spots with pick-ups."

He waved his hand airily. "Don't give it a thought, my boy. I'm in no danger as yet."

The dining room was fairly crowded with a well-dressed, animated group of people. As we ate our excellent dinner, I noticed glances of approval toward the aristocratic figure seated opposite me. His fellow-diners hadn't heard him making the date with the waitress. You had to be fairly intimate with the Colonel to get that smell the chief had noticed.

Dinner finished, the Colonel offered me a cigar. "Glad to see you take that, my boy," he said approvingly. "The pipe is all very well for the ranks, but just between ourselves, a cigar is the thing for an officer and a gentleman. Not that I'm not democratic, mind you, but there is a certain line we must draw." Nobody else could have gotten away with a remark like that without sounding a complete fool.

I grinned at him. "I was a sergeant in the late unpleasantness, Colonel. And just to remind you that you after all did hire a detective, I'll add that at least I was in the army."

"True enough, Jonathan, true enough. You are a detective. If I also might make a statement for the record, your present assignment is to prevent future dangers, not make impertinent speculations on my past." He wasn't sore — at least he didn't show it — and his ruddy old poker face wasn't giving away a thing. There might have been a twinkle in his eye. I never did entirely make up my mind about the Colonel's sense of humor.

"You can't always separate them. Men have been found in a New York alley with their throats cut because they slapped a waitress in Kansas City. Not that you would do a thing like that, but you see what I mean."

He beamed at me. "Very well, my boy, speculate to your heart's content, and I'm sure you will keep me in perfect health. Shall we go now?"

CHAPTER TWO

THERE WERE few people in the lobby as we left the dining room and approached the elevator. I had no reason to notice particularly the man who had been standing with his back to us, apparently studying the floor indicator, until he whirled suddenly and held out his hand to the Colonel.

"Hello Colonel," he said. "Fancy meeting you here." At the same time, two other figures closed in on us. One of them, a hulking brute who could have snapped my neck with a twist of his wrists, put an arm lovingly across my shoulders and said: "How you doing, boy? Any pal of the Colonel's is a pal of mine." The third man stood slightly aside, hands thrust in his coat pockets. It was as neat and complete a trap as I had ever seen sprung, though to the by-standers it must have appeared to be a sudden meeting of old friends.

The Colonel settled one question I had often speculated on — how he would act when the chips were down. His face showed no emotion at all, but he took the outstretched hand and pumped it vigorously. "Hart, old man, it's good to see you again."

"How about asking us up for a drink, Colonel?"

"Certainly, certainly. Step right in the elevator with us."

We rode in silence to the top floor. I recognized Lucky Hart, an Eastern gambler with the reputation of being a bad man to fool around with, although we had never come in personal contact before. The torpedo holding the guns on us from his pockets was Eddie Titano, also with a record. The big gorilla still hugging me in the rock-crusher embrace was a new one to me. I leaned against him from enough angles to convince myself he wasn't carrying a gun.

We went into our rooms — we had a sitting room, bedroom and bath — just like that. Once inside, the big lug took his hands off me and stepped back, giving me a not unfriendly grin. The torpedo kept his attention centered on the Colonel. I saw that they hadn't recognized me and weren't figuring me for much of a part in what was to come. It gave me a chance to size up the gathering.

Lucky Hart was perhaps thirty-five, slight of build, dark-featured, not unhandsome. He had a gambler's expressionless face. A bulge under one arm showed that he carried a gun. Titano was a very small man — the body of an undeveloped high school boy, with a face that was a lot older than that.

He had the reputation of being a hop-head, but there was no indication of the stuff on him then. The big fellow had a twisted left ear, lumpy eyebrows, the general look of an ex-fighter or wrestler gone to seed.

"Colonel," Hart was saying in a flat, even tone, "that was a pretty good little card game we had back in Jersey, wasn't it?"

The old boy actually smiled at him. "Very fine, yes, indeed. I enjoyed it greatly."

"I'll bet you did. But I'm surprised at you, Colonel. I've looked you up since, and your record doesn't run like that. Weren't you getting a little out of line, playing the wise money for suckers?"

"Bless my soul, what a way to express it. You gentlemen were kind enough to invite me into a small, friendly game, and I accepted. Good fortune was with me. You yourself suggested raising the stakes."

"Yeah, I know. We picked you for just what you were claiming to be — a rich old sucker. It was a damned public place, so the laugh was on us. Understand, I'm not squawking. I just thought you might like to roll the bones with me. Maybe only one roll, for say twenty grand." Hart took a pair of dice from his pocket and flipped them out on the table. A five and a two turned up. "No sudden moves, Colonel," he added sharply. "Remember, that time in Frisco you were just a little too sudden for your own good. That's why I brought Eddie here along — to save you from any more of that kind of embarrassment."

That last part gave me something to think about. It suggested an angle to the Colonel I hadn't really considered, and it surprised me.

No one was even looking at me. All eyes were on the Colonel as he stood there thoughtfully stroking his mustache. I sauntered a couple of paces to one side, putting myself almost squarely behind the torpedo, but where I had a clear view of Lucky Hart. Then with a flip of the wrist I had my gun on them.

"Don't turn around, Eddie," I said conversationally. "Lift those hands out slow and careful and hold them high. That goes for all of you."

It is always interesting to watch a man's reactions at a time like that, especially if you are in a good spot yourself. Lucky Hart looked momentarily startled, but recovered himself almost at once. He took a quick look at the Mauser cradled in my palm and immediately put up his hands, nodding to Titano to do the same. The little guy didn't take it quite so calmly. He began to shake and jerk, so that for a moment I was set for trouble, but gradually his hands came out of the pockets and up. The gorilla looked dazed with astonishment. His hands were up fast enough to please anyone, though.

The Colonel gave me the real surprise. At the first sound of my voice his right hand flicked into his left sleeve, and he stood there covering them with as ugly a little double-barreled derringer as I ever saw. The old guy had certainly been holding out on me. He must have been packing that sleeve gun for the last two weeks, without it ever having occurred to me. In fact, I hadn't figured anyone had carried a sleeve gun since 1900.

I came up behind Titano to lift a .45 automatic from each coat pocket. They were almost as big as he was, and must have made his clothes sag like anything when his hands weren't on them. Then I circled and took a neat little .32 short-barreled revolver from Hart. I started to skip the big boy, but remembering the Colonel's sleeve gun, I patted him carefully. He was clean.

"Now gentlemen," the Colonel said politely, "were you really interested in some game of chance?"

Hart ignored him, staring hard at me. "Apparently I didn't do quite enough checking," he said, no malice or excitement showing in his voice. "I place you now, friend. You're Jonny Marks of the Watson Agency. What are you doing as a hired gun for a small-time card sharp? I didn't think Watson handled that kind of stuff."

He had me there — I couldn't quite figure it out myself. The Colonel answered for me. "Jonathan is handling another matter for me at present. This is entirely in addition to his regular duties."

"Well, it's your move," Hart said flatly. "What do you aim to do with us? Not that you'll get away with this in the long run."

I punched the shells from his gun, took the magazines from the torpedo's automatics, and flipped them back to the owners. "We're putting you out right now," I said. "Don't come back while I'm working for the Colonel. After that you can cut each other's throats to your hearts' content. And you might be interested to know I'm phoning a report of this little deal in to the agency tonight."

"Not interested," Hart said calmly. "I've no feud with your boys, Marks, though I will be having twenty grand from the Colonel one of these days."

He put his gun away and went out the door, his two stooges following. Titano gave me a long, black look as he left. The big fellow winked at me.

The Colonel tested the lock on the door and turned to me. "Excellent, my boy, excellent. I see that I wasn't mistaken in my confidence in you." He might have been speaking of a hand of bridge. He went over to the sofa and settled himself comfortably, drawing a fresh cigar from his pigskin cigar case.

"It won't do, Colonel. The time has come for us to have a little talk."

"Certainly, Jonathan, anything at all."

"No, just one thing. I want to know where I stand. What am I hired for?

Hart wasn't kidding when he said the Watson agency had a legitimate reputation. I don't mind bucking him in any on-the-level deal, but the boss will
never okay stringing along on either side of a card sharp war."

"Jonathan, you pain me deeply. I give you my word that this affair this
evening was a complete surprise to me, having no connection with the matter for which you were employed. Still, I can make no apology for winning
the twenty thousand dollars from Lucky Hart. It was my good fortune to be
holding phenomenal cards that evening, while at times I had the impression
Mr. Hart and his associates were not being entirely legitimate in their
methods."

I had to grin at that. "That I can believe, Colonel. There must have
been times when six or seven aces were floating around that game. But you
haven't been leveling with me, you must admit. I didn't even know you
were packing a gun. And what did he mean by that Frisco crack?"

"A very old affair, my boy. The actions of an impetuous youth. That
again has no connection with our present plans. You have my word as an
officer and a gentleman that I am at present engaged in a legitimate business
enterprise of considerable magnitude, the nature of which I am not at liberty to divulge. Certain unscrupulous characters may well attempt to interfere. That is my sole reason for employing you."

I let it go at that, and sat there in silence for a time, mentally reviewing
what I knew of the Colonel.

He had come into our agency in New York a couple of weeks before, a
bluff, prosperous figure with a confidence-inspiring manner. He made a
reasonably good first impression always — it was closer acquaintance which
told you things about him. He gave a straightforward, fairly believable
story. He said he was a retired army man with extensive business interests,
that he was approaching the climax of a deal which he feared rivals might
try to block. He wanted to hire a man with three qualifications: ability to
wear clothes well and pass as his secretary; ability physically to handle unexpected trouble; and ability to carry on with the case to insure legal evidence necessary for a conviction in the event the Colonel himself should be
killed. He paid the robust fee required of him without protest. The chief
ignored the clothes angle entirely, and assigned me.

Since that time observation had taught me a bit more about him. I dis-
counted the retired army officer story entirely. He might or might not
have served a brief period as either an officer or enlisted man — about sixty
now, he could have been in the First World War — but I was convinced
that he had never been a professional soldier.

Neither did I believe that he actually possessed those "large financial
interests." We had come west by easy stages, stopping several days in

Chicago and Detroit. Both during the stops and on the train the Colonel played cards continually, for as large stakes as he could manage without departing from his role of a tired business man seeking recreation. Bridge and poker were his specialties, and he always won, unspectacularly but steadily. He never suggested that I play, but I had watched enough to be convinced that he was an artist, in a dishonest sort of way.

In short, I had become convinced that the Colonel was just about what Lucky Hart called him — a small-time card sharp. But what was I doing there? His winnings, while considerable, were far from being enough to pay both our expenses and settle the agency fee as well.

I doubted that he was accustomed to spending money at his present rate, or to moving in the circles he loved to discuss. A dozen little things gave it away. He was not really familiar with wearing evening clothes; for all his formal language he was not entirely at ease in any prolonged conversation with people who could toss those five-dollar words back at him. Possibly the type of women he genuinely seemed to prefer told a story also, although you can go overboard on a deduction like that.

Of course, he might just be having a spree with his unusual winnings from Hart, but where did I fit in a picture like that? He couldn't hope to carry me around the rest of his life to protect him from the gangster.

The Colonel was an open book to me in many isolated instances, but the total effect when I tried to put the pieces together was as of a blank page. Too many things like that unexpected gun kept throwing me for a loss.

Another incongruous feature was that at heart he was a kindly man. One night in Chicago a game of stud poker in our room that began as the usual "friendly game" gradually became steep. A white-faced youngster emptied his pockets and eventually wrote a check for two hundred dollars. His shaking fingers made it pretty obvious that he did not have the money in the bank. The Colonel called him back as the others left, gave him a pompous little lecture on playing beyond his means, and tore up the check!

I decided to telegraph a full report to the chief and let him do the worrying. I went downstairs and sent the telegram from a booth in the lobby. I suggested that if we stayed on the case we have a man in Frisco check up on any old shooting scrape which might give us a line on the Colonel.

CHAPTER THREE

WE ACTUALLY did meet the two waitresses at ten-fifteen. I protested, both because I didn't feel it possible to keep an adequate eye on the Colonel during a round of night clubs and because it seemed to me we could do better than that. The old boy insisted, however, and by eleven o'clock we were established at a prominent table in a joint called the Club Factor.

The blonde, Mabel by name, was about as I expected. A little too much make-up, her voice a shade loud for my taste, she was nevertheless good-natured, friendly, and fitted into the atmosphere of the place well enough. Obviously she considered the Colonel a prize catch and was pleased to be seen with him.

Vera, the red-head, was inclined to be difficult. She was a good-looking girl, or had the makings of one, but like the Colonel himself she didn't stand close inspection too well. Her brilliant fingernail polish was chipped at several points; her leg makeup was slightly streaky. The white collar she affected was minutely soiled. And she was very determined to show that, while she might go out with strange men, she certainly wasn't the type to allow anyone to make a pass at her.

She got this impression across during our first dance. Previous to that I hadn't been able to get much of a line on her attitude, her remarks being limited to a cold "Pleased to meetcha" when Mabel introduced us, and an improbable-sounding "Delighted" when I asked her to dance.

She held her back muscles very stiff under my hand and kept about three inches farther away from me than propriety demanded. She wasn't sore — that was just her version of the proper way to act the first time a gentleman took you out. Under my breath I cursed the Colonel wholeheartedly and completely.

He was circling the dance floor with Mabel clinging as tightly to him as plaster on the wall. Even under those circumstances he managed to look jovially dignified, a gentleman slumming for the evening.

Back at the table, the Colonel hospitably poured the champagne he had ordered. It wasn't champagne in the strict sense of the word, but the name alone gave Vera a considerable feeling of elegance. She seemed to like it, tossing off one glass and generously allowing the Colonel to refill it.

"I don't really drink," she explained. "Only light wines like this." That was her longest speech of the evening to date. It gave me an uneasy qualm.

I was none too sure what the stuff was, but definitely it was not light wine.

"Dance with me, big boy," Mabel commanded. "I never danced with a secretary before. I thought they were all dames." The red-head, having finished her second glass, laughed immoderately at this sally.

Mabel's code did not require stiffness. She said chummily: "This is gonna be a real party. I bet your boss is some sport when he gets going." I had an idea she might be right.

I was disappointed to see that the Colonel and Vera weren't dancing, as it might have been interesting to see how their two styles mingled. All the action I could see at the table was the Colonel filling Vera's glass.

Mabel noticed too, giggling appreciatively. "The Colonel has the right idea, big boy. Liquor doesn't change me much, but when Vera gets to drinking, she's a card."

After the dance, the girls excused themselves and headed for the rest-room. As they passed by the bar, I saw a thin, middle-aged man in a pin-stripe suit speak to Mabel for a moment. She nodded, patted his cheek absently, and passed on. I started to say something to the Colonel, but he carefully evaded my eyes while he beat time with his fingers to the blaring music.

"All right," I said, "you needn't look so blasted innocent. It's your evening and your neck. I'm not saying anything."

After the girls returned, Vera persuaded herself to have a couple more soft drinks. Then she looked me straight in the eye and said, "Dance?" And she winked at me slowly and sensually. I said, "Delighted."

Either the wine or the time element seemed to have dissolved the need for formality on her part. She pressed a slightly moist cheek hard against mine and draped her body limply on me. Her left arm was curled around my neck. She was not exactly my dream girl, but she was feminine and not bad-looking and I had taken some of that synthetic champagne myself. I enjoyed the dance, except for a lock of violently scented red hair which kept brushing against my nose.

After the dance we found Mabel busily applying lipstick. "We're going to the Club Arbor," she said. "This joint's dead."

"Right-o," the Colonel agreed. "On with the dance, and all that sort of thing." During the course of the evening he had picked up an increasingly marked English accent.

The Club Arbor proved to be just outside the city limits. It stood on a low hill not far off the highway. The yard was jammed with cars and there seemed to be a crowd, but I was vaguely uneasy. I slipped a bill in the driver's hand and told him to wait.

Inside, it was like any second-rate night club, more crowded and a bit noisier than the one we had just left. The only justification for the name "Arbor" was a sprinkling of papier-mâché trees at either side of the bandstand. The Colonel demanded, and received after the passage of a bill, a table on the edge of the dance floor. A five-piece orchestra was really giving out, producing volume if nothing else.

"Scotch and soda, my man," the Colonel told the waiter. I expected to hear him start reciting Kipling next, and discussing the white man's burden. The girls said Scotch and soda would be fine with them. I ordered straight Bourbon.

Vera had two drinks before we danced. I immediately felt a change in her attitude — the back muscles were stiff again. "I'm a good sport," she said coldly, "but don't keep getting so fresh." I sensed that a continued policy of mixing Vera's drinks might create a problem before the evening was over.

As we danced on the far side of the room from our table, I caught sight of the man in the pin-striped suit bending over a table against the wall. Whatever he was saying didn't take long, and he disappeared through a door almost hidden by one of the fake trees. I looked closely at the two occupants of the table. They were both young, both big-boned and rugged-looking. One of them had a broken nose. They were fairly well-dressed and did not seem to be drinking.

I told Vera I wanted to sit the next dance out. I was disturbed, without quite knowing why, by the reappearance of the man in the pin-stripe suit and by his two capable-looking acquaintances. A careful study of the room showed no other suspicious characters. A big, hard-boiled-appearing man whom I took to be the bouncer leaned against the wall near the entrance. It was the sort of place to have an obvious bouncer.

Vera petulantly reached out and took the glass of Bourbon the waiter had just brought me. "Why don't you get me one of these? Are you too cheap to spend any money on me?" With elaborate care, she poured her own drink on the floor.

"Now, honey," Mabel said soothingly, "take it easy. We all want to have fun."

"Boy," the Colonel shouted, clapping his hands. "Straight Bourbon for the mem-sahib."

"Don't you call me names!" Vera almost yelled.

"Now, honey, the Colonel is just getting you a nice drink. The Colonel is a sweetheart." Mabel was definitely a peacemaker.

"All right," Vera sniffed, looking ready to cry. "It's just that everybody is so mean to me."

"Madame," the Colonel said gallantly, "you wrong me. Will you do me the honor of having this dance with me?"

"Delighted." She gave me a dirty look as they left.

"That's one trouble with Vera on a party," Mabel said apologetically. "After a while she starts to get sore."

Vera and the Colonel were attempting a samba in the middle of the room when it happened. She stepped back from him with a scream so high and shrill that the orchestra stopped in mid-beat, and slapped his face. "He insulted me!" she yelled.

At the same time the big figure of the bouncer loomed up beside me, his hand clamping down on my right arm with an iron grip. "Sit right where you are," he told me.

The two huskies were rushing out from their table against the wall, while from the corner of my eye I saw Pin-Stripe heading into it from the entrance way. Every customer in the place was staring, and the couples closest to the Colonel and Vera were backing away.

I turned to gaze up at the bouncer, trying to look even more startled than I felt. While our eyes met, my left hand found the neck of a bottle of beer Mabel had fancied for a chaser. I swept it up and over my shoulder and heard a satisfying thud as it caught him just beside the ear. I started for the middle of the room, feeling sure he was out of the play for a time, at least.

Now I have never been one of those characters who can hit a man one short jolt to the jaw and feel confident he will fade. Generally, in fact, I can bang away at him for some time and he will still have enough steam to put me away. Still, there are always ways and means, so in the few short steps before I hit the edge of the mob, my black-jack was out of my hip pocket and fitted snugly in my left hand.

Pin-Stripe was shoving his way through just ahead of me. Acting on the theory that he might be in the deal and certainly wouldn't be on our side, I reached out and tapped him scientifically. All eyes being on the principals, no one even noticed him slide gently to the floor.

Breaking through the last of the crowd, I saw that Broken-nose was holding the Colonel firmly from behind, while his pal stood menacingly in front of the old boy.

"Insult a lady, will you?" the second man was growling. "I'm going to fix you so you won't insult anyone for a while."

Meanwhile Vera kept screaming, "He insulted me!" It was undoubtedly a frame-up, but I had to admit to myself that she was probably telling the truth, at that.

Just before the knight errant could hit the Colonel, I was behind him, parting his hair neatly with the black-jack. Slugging a man from behind may not be heroic, but it is quick and efficient and you can judge your force very nicely. He was out like a light, without my having to worry about his being seriously hurt. Vera stopped screaming to stare at me.

Broken-nose dropped the Colonel's arms as soon as he saw me in the play and started around him to get at me. He came with his hands out in front of him, fists open and fingers spread, like a wrestler, and I knew that if he got those hands on me it would be curtains. I didn't want to pull a gun, so I got set to try for a quick finish with the black-jack.

I needn't have bothered. As he passed in front of the Colonel, that gentleman raised his left arm and slammed it down over the top of the wrestler's head. Knowing what was in that sleeve, I wasn't surprised to see Broken-nose join his pal on the floor.

I slipped the Mauser out from under my arm and into my right hand coat pocket, keeping my hand on it there. By that time the sap was back in my pocket, and I doubt if any of the open-mouthed bystanders realized it hadn't been done by sheer manly dexterity.

"Let's get out of here," I said. "Somebody is always starting a fight in these dives."

"Right-o, my boy. Not the place for a gentleman," the Colonel agreed calmly. "Coming, my dear?" This last to a now quiet Vera.

Mabel joined us at the door, and we made the waiting cab before any of our playmates put in an appearance.

CHAPTER FOUR

I AWOKE THE next morning to the usual unmelodious rumble of the Colonel's snores. He lay on his back, mouth open, mustache limp and bedraggled. As I watched him, the snores gargled to a stop and he opened one eye.

"Good morning, Jonathan. Beautiful Sabbath morning, is it not?"

"Where is the English accent this morning?" I asked nastily. "Last night you were really beating the drums of Empire."

"I have served a good deal with our British cousins, and have perhaps picked up some of their mannerisms." His voice was as smooth as butter. "How is your head this morning, my boy? I seem to recall that you drank rather heavily last evening."

"I drank heavily!" I said bitterly. "How did you have time to watch me, the way you were pouring it down that Vera? I hope she has a hangover this morning."

"There would seem little doubt that she will have. But tell me, Jonathan, was it your impression that the young lady's performance was entirely spontaneous?"

So he had kept his eyes open. I told him about the man speaking to Mabel earlier in the evening, who had subsequently showed up at the Club Arbor talking with the two strong-arm boys.

"Though I'm not at all sure Vera was just putting on an act. She strikes me as too dumb. She was really fairly drunk, unless she has the capacity of a camel, and she had already passed through the loving stage and was starting to get tough."

"What is your considered opinion of the incident as a whole?" he asked.

"It was a frame-up, certainly. The Arbor management must have been in on it, because the bouncer tried to keep me out at the start. They had no idea of killing you, I think. The place was too public and they moved too slow. They just meant to beat you up good and leave you there. It was pretty well planned, at that. You weren't in any position to make much of a beef afterwards. It would just go down as a drunken brawl."

The colonel nodded his head, but slowly, as though to keep his eyes from dropping out. I got the impression that he was relieved to find me in agreement with his own theories. I also began to realize he was dragging out the conversation largely because he didn't feel like sitting up.

"I believe you are right, Jonathan. Well, it's a small matter. Nothing to interfere with our more important plans. I'm sure it has no connection with my mission here." He swung his legs out of bed.

"You mean you intend to leave it at that? Not me. A little talk with Mabel, now that she is sober, should put me on to the track of our friend in the flashy clothes. I think he had her take us to the Club Arbor. A few well chosen words with him might help us find out who was behind it. I have a hunch it was intended as a sort of warning from Lucky Hart."

"No, Jonathan, definitely no. You are probably right about Hart — it doesn't matter. I don't want to spend any time or effort on these unimportant details. Whatever the reason for last night, it has no connection with my real business here. I'm sure of that. In any event, I have other plans for this afternoon.'

I gave up. I didn't even ask him the plans for the afternoon. I just reached over to the stand beside the bed for my pipe, and had the satisfaction of seeing him shudder as the first puff of smoke went up to the ceiling. "How about some ham and eggs for breakfast, Colonel?" I asked him.

Again the shudder. "Thank you, my boy, no. A glass of tomato juice and a cup of coffee will be sufficient. Really, you know, the constitution of youth won't last forever."

"Depends on how you live," I said smugly, reaching for the telephone. "Never drink too much, never have hangovers." Actually I was far from feeling as good as all that. "Two cups of coffee, two glasses of tomato juice, one double order of ham and eggs," I told room service.

That did it. The Colonel headed for the bathroom, a slightly greenish tinge overlying the usual purple of his complexion. The look he fixed on me as he went through the door was baleful.

When he came out from his shower, his outward aplomb was entirely restored, however he may have felt inwardly. Dressed solely in a suit of athletic shorts, which made his figure one of the world's lesser marvels, he planted himself before the mirror and carefully waxed his mustache. It was, as always, a labor of love which he did not hurry. Satisfied at last with its spiked elegance, he turned and beamed at me.

"No breakfast yet, Jonathan?"

I dragged deeply on the pipe. "No, they're slow as ever. But that's okay — I like a long smoke before breakfast."

He had the stomach under control by then — I suspected the bottle of Scotch he kept in the bathroom. His smile widened genially as he carefully eased his undershirt over his head, making quite a proposition of it to avoid disturbing the mustache. Next he put on a white shirt with a wing collar, of a sort I'd never in my life seen aside from newsreels of fashionable weddings. Even in the newsreels I never saw one worn with white flannel pants and a double-breasted blue serge coat. That was what he put on, though, above black and white sport shoes of loud design. He added a pearl grey four-in-hand tie which stopped just short of being an ascot. When I saw that get-up, I knew he was set for something big. I had seen him wear it only once before, at a hotel in Detroit when he allowed a couple of would-be sharpshooters to teach him to play five-card stud.

He signified that he was fully dressed by carefully shooting his cuffs to display to advantage the outsize pearl links he had picked up in that Detroit game. They looked too big to be real, and I told him so. He looked pained.

"Dear me, I hope they are real. I hazarded a considerable sum of money against them, you will recall."

Breakfast came then, wheeled in by a leering bellboy who had unquestionably heard something of last night's date with Mabel and Vera. "Put it over there," I told him, "and don't let your imagination run away with you." He just looked at me. I never saw a kid who could cram so much indecent speculation into a look. I flipped a quarter to him and settled myself to the ham and eggs.

"What's on today, Colonel?" I asked.

"Nothing at all, my boy. Nothing in a business way, that is. I plan to pay a purely social call. I thought you might care to browse about the town a bit."

"Maybe I better just browse along with you," I suggested. "Something tells me this climate isn't healthy for you. I'll try not to ruin you socially — I have a clean shirt."

But he didn't go for it. He began by complimenting me on my conscientious regard for my duty, and grew solicitous over my lack of leisure, but when you boiled it all down, the only thing he had said was that he didn't want me along.

As soon as I got the drift I started tossing my clothes on, making it as casual as possible. I phoned the desk to call him a cab, and told the clerk to send the boy to get the dishes and bring a morning paper right away. I emphasized the "right away."

"Dick Tracy's in a jam," I explained to the Colonel. "I just remembered this is Sunday. And twelve o'clock Sunday is no time to go calling," I added.

He didn't even give me an answer to that, but just went back into the bathroom. He was really leaning into that Scotch, even for him.

The bellhop who came for the tray was the same one who had brought it up, and he was still leering at me. He looked about sixteen but must have been older. No kid could learn that much in sixteen years.

"You got a car?" I asked him.

He dropped the leer to look insulted. "How you think I get to work —

the streetcar?"

"How would you like to take me for a little ride?"

He looked at me pityingly. I'm just not the type to inspire much respect in bellboys or head waiters. "I'm working, bud," he said.

"You could get sick, couldn't you?" I showed him a ten-dollar bill.

"Yeah, I'm not feeling so hot right now. Where you want to go? Sir —" he added, taking another look at the bill.

"You be parked out front in five minutes, no more. Have a hat and coat on over that monkey suit. Don't look too close at anyone but me. Get it?"

"I get it." He reached for the ten dollars, which I put back in my pocket. "That you get later. Now beat it."

He gathered up the dishes and left just as the Colonel came out of the bathroom. "A bright lad," the old hypocrite commented. "Makes one feel certain of the future of America."

"He does at that. I wouldn't be a bit surprised to see that boy follow right in your footsteps, Colonel."

I managed to hold him for ten minutes or so in random conversation and then let him go without further protest. He left me sitting in an easy chair, pipe going full blast and the funny papers scattered around me. Once I heard the elevator going down, I didn't stay there long.

The kid was parked right where I told him to be, slouched behind the wheel of a robin's-egg blue Buick convertible. I swore a little to myself — it was about as inconspicuous as a fire engine. I waited in the lobby until a yellow cab with the Colonel in it pulled away from the curb; then I made for the Buick.

"Keep that cab in sight," I told the kid. "Stay about half a block —"

"I been to the movies," he said coldly. "You don't need to draw me a picture." He was excited, though, and his blasé pose couldn't quite hide it. He got the Buick away fast, driving as though he knew what he was doing.

It was one of those bright yet cool summer days which seem to be a Pacific Coast specialty. Our hotel was in the University district, a locality which managed to give a pleasantly rural impression while keeping most urban advantages. There wasn't much traffic, but enough so that we could keep a car or so between us and the cab and still have it well in view.

We followed them out of the business district and onto the bluff overlooking the bay. It was a locality of really fine homes, the grounds of each occupying a half-block or more of space. It was hard to imagine the Colonel being on drop-in terms with the owner of one of those estates. Even the kid was impressed.

I motioned him to pull up and stop, still a block behind, when the cab drew up in front of a three-story red brick affair with several acres of windows. I whipped a pair of small field glasses from my pocket and trained them on the door of the house.

We watched the Colonel pay the driver and walk up to the entrance. The man who answered his ring was not my notion of what a butler should look like, but that seemed to be his function. He was a hard-faced, granite-jawed party, something above middle height and quite a bit above middle shoulder breadth. Those shoulders were as square across as a drill sergeant's. He had the mean, suspicious eye of a drill sergeant, too, and I was rather inclined to dislike him on the spot. If I had been casting the picture, he would have been the retired army man and the Colonel would have been the butler. I put the glasses away, not liking the look he threw toward us over the Colonel's shoulder. Though it would have taken good eyes to have picked up the glasses at that distance, considering the way I was crouched down in the seat.

After the door closed behind the Colonel, the kid and I sat there and swapped lies for maybe thirty minutes. He told me his name was Jerry, which was very likely the truth, but from there on he branched out into stuff he must have been making up as he went along. Not that he wouldn't have been capable of it, given time, but it would have taken fifty years to crowd in that much gambling, fornication, bootlegging and white slavery, to say nothing of a hitch in the marines he threw in for good measure. I told him I was a special agent for a Congressional Committee investigating gambling on the West Coast, and he didn't believe me either.

We were sitting there, having a pretty good time in our own way, when a shadow dropped across us from behind and I felt a hand on my right shoulder. "No sudden moves," someone growled at us.

I turned my head slowly, as requested, and there stood the hard-faced butler. He was holding my shoulder with his left hand — the right was buried in his pocket. I had no way of knowing for sure what that pocket held, but if it was a gun, it was in a fine position to blow me right in two. I said hello in a carefully non-provocative tone.

"What's your racket?" the butler asked. He didn't sound like any butler I ever heard in the movies.

"No racket — we just like to drive around and see how you rich guys live. No harm in that, is there?" I tried to put a small amount of indignant taxpayer in my voice, without downright offending him. So far as I was concerned, he was holding the book of rules for this game right in his pocket.

He let go my arm. "Better keep driving, then. And keep those glasses to yourself. We don't like peeping Toms around here."

"Yes sir," I said. I motioned to Jerry, which was all he had been waiting for. He slammed his foot on the starter and got out of there.

"Brother," I said as we rounded the corner, "I was a little scared. But I don't suppose it meant a thing to you, after Korea."

He gave me a bitter look. "Wise guy, aren't you?" he commented, heading back for the hotel.

It took me a lot of talk and another ten dollars to get him turned around and parked a couple of blocks up the street and around a corner, where we could use the glasses on the front door from behind some shrubs. He insisted on the ten in advance, too.

For the next hour the conversation was hardly so sprightly. Jerry spent most of his time looking on all sides and behind for more unexpected company, while I had my own mental problems. I didn't like leaving the Colonel in that house alone. On the other hand, in view of his specific desire to go by himself, I didn't quite know how to go about getting him out. And there was always the chance, maybe even the probability, that the old scoundrel was embroiled in something there that the agency would want no part of. I decided just to sit tight for a while, trusting in the Colonel's wits and his sleeve gun.

It turned out all right. When the Colonel did come out, he appeared to be in as good shape as ever. Better, in fact, because he had a girl with him. It was too far for me to get a really good look at her, but she walked with a light, youthful swing and I judged the Colonel was satisfied. They went into the three-car garage at the side of the house, presently reappearing in a snappy two-tone club coupé, the girl driving. I gave Jerry the nod to follow them.

The coupé was headed in the general direction of the University district, so I took a chance. "Beat them to the hotel," I told Jerry. "I think you're well enough to get back to work."

My hunch paid off. Thanks to Jerry's driving, which scared me a lot more than any of his stories, I was standing at the cigar counter in the lobby when the Colonel and the girl pulled up in front. I took a really good look at her then, and she was worth it.

About twenty-two, hair with the sheen of yellow silk, and eyes the exact shade of the soft blue sweater she was wearing. She was laughing at something the Colonel said, and as he got out of the car she held out her hand. He bent over it gallantly, not kissing it, but holding her fingers till she pulled them away.

I expected to see him come swinging into the hotel with a conquering swagger, possibly twirling his mustache. I was wrong. He came in slowly, his mouth slack and dispirited, his hands limp at his sides. He looked like a tired old man. He gave me a nod and the smallest suggestion of a smile before he headed for the elevator. I followed him up to the room.

Once inside, he dropped down in a chair, not even bothering to lift his pants at the knees to protect the crease. For him, that spelled something catastrophic. My natural impulse to needle him had died when he walked through that hotel door — there was definitely something wrong with the Colonel. I went into the bathroom to get his private bottle of Scotch, pouring out about three fingers in a bathroom glass.

"Thank you, Marks," he said, downing it neatly. "I needed that." It was the first time he had ever called me solely by my last name.

I sat down on the couch and hauled out my pipe, simulating an elaborate interest in the scene from the window. There was something indecent in looking at the old man as he sat there with all his ridiculous pretensions so thoroughly gone. When I finally did look at him, he was sitting watching me, a tight, bitter smile that was almost a parody of his usual jovial beam twisting his mouth under the trim mustache.

"Don't mind me, Marks. It's just that I've given myself a shock. We all have our little weaknesses, and I've just run onto one of mine. It has upset all my calculations."

I didn't say anything. He poured another generous slug, swallowed it, and went on: "Yes, I've always pretty well agreed with your opinion of me. You weren't exactly flattering, but I felt you understood me very well. Now it seems that you and I were both wrong. I do have my decent moments, after all. It is disconcerting, to say the least."

I didn't say anything. What is there to say to a speech like that?

"At any rate," he went on, "my plans have been altered. Our association, pleasant though it is" — some of the old pompous quality was creeping back — "will be ending. You are free to return to New York any time you chose."

"Look, Colonel," I said, "I'm not trying to pry into your affairs. If you say I'm through, the time for prying is past. But I don't want to leave you alone in this town. It's a bad spot for you." Speaking of being surprised at yourself, that remark was something of a shock to me. I would have told anyone, two hours before, that the Colonel was strictly business with me, and that once he was no longer my responsibility I wouldn't give a damn if someone treated him as he no doubt thoroughly deserved. Now I found that wasn't entirely true. I was actually worried about the old pirate.

"Very well, Marks. There is no cause for concern, but it is very good of you to take the interest." I think he was really pleased, although the guard was coming back up and he was never an easy man to read. "At any rate, there is nothing to keep me here. Perhaps you will be good enough to arrange for a reservation to" — he hesitated for a brief moment — "St.

Petersburg, Florida.

"Okay, Colonel. I'll see you off before I go myself."

The Colonel hesitated again before speaking — for perhaps the first time since I had met him he appeared faintly embarrassed. "By the way, Jonathan," he finally got out, "a simple lower berth will be ample for my needs. I won't be a particularly large scale operator for a time."

"Sure, Colonel. I'll go pick it up now." I wanted to get out of there, to give the old man a chance to re-build his morale fences by himself.

"And, Jonathan, I won't be needing you this evening. I promise not to go out — I'll even have dinner sent up here to me. You might as well enjoy yourself for once."

I didn't argue with him. He was in that frame of mind which makes solitude a necessity to a man. He wanted to be alone, and I had no desire to stay around and bother him. I just answered with a nod and walked out without saying anything else to him. I never did say anything else to him.

I killed the rest of the afternoon by sending a telegram to the chief, making our reservations, and dropping in at a newsreel theater. The last was strictly nothing but an expedient for spending time because I didn't want to disturb the Colonel. I ate at a small restaurant a couple of blocks from the hotel, not caring to resume relationship of any sort with Vera and Mabel right at the moment.

My interest in Colonel Alexander Smallwood was officially dead. Unofficially, I retained enough to make me get a city directory to look up the address of the house where the Colonel spent the afternoon. It belonged to Thornton Caldwell, who lived there with his wife Janet and his daughter Antonia. The names meant nothing to me.

CHAPTER FIVE

IT WAS ABOUT eight o'clock when I finally returned to the hotel. Still not too anxious to confront the Colonel, I dropped in at the tap room. Since it was Sunday, nothing alcoholic was officially sold, but signs said that soft drinks were available. A few couples were dancing to the juke box. There were glasses on the bar and on the tables in the booths which didn't look like soft drinks to me.

"Give me a coke," I told the bartender, "with a small shot of Bourbon in it."

"Yes, sir," he answered, and proceeded to mix the drink without comment. Maybe he recognized me as a guest of the hotel; maybe he just didn't care. He couldn't have figured me for a cop, because he charged me fifty cents.

A couple in the booth just across from me caught my attention as I sat there idly nursing the Bourbon and coke. The man was a big, red-haired young fellow, possibly a couple of years younger than I. That would make him about twenty-seven. The girl was the Colonel's chauffeur of the afternoon.

I got a better chance to study her then, and she was still worth the trouble. Her hair was still shining, even out of the sunlight. Her skin was clear, and a smooth, warm tan against the white sharkskin suit she was wearing. She had a jeweled green bauble on her left lapel, and while I am no expert on such matters, it didn't look to me like the sort of thing you pick up at the costume jewelry counter in a department store. She looked expensive, and she also looked mad — that showed in every line of her face and in the swift, stabbing gestures with which she ground out her cigarette. The red-head was evidently trying to talk her out of something, but I got the impression that he wasn't going over. Eventually she drained her glass and rose abruptly, walking out into the lobby. He shrugged his shoulders and beckoned to the bartender.

Our eyes met briefly. He hesitated, giving me the tentative grin of a man who is often recognized by people whom he doesn't know.

When the bartender came back, I said casually: "I seem to have met that big fellow somewhere. Who is he?"

"Tom Pierce," was the prompt answer. "Best fullback we ever had here at the U. I guess maybe you have seen him somewhere."

I picked up my glass and sauntered over to the booth. "How does the team look this year?" I asked.

His glum face brightened perceptibly. "Not bad, not bad at all. I've been working out some with the boys this summer, and I like the looks of it." He motioned to the bench opposite him. "Sit down —" he hesitated, searching for my name.

"I'm Jonny Marks," I said. "You wouldn't remember me. I was just a sub. I came over because I've seen you in action from the bench, but never got a chance to meet you."

He looked pleased. "Hell, I wasn't so much. What school?"

"Stanford," I said, because that was the first name that occurred to me. I hoped the conversation wasn't going to involve technicalities which my experience in a seat on the fifty-yard line couldn't handle.

"Say, you boys really had it back there. It took a good man to get on that travelling squad. Especially as light as you are."

I guess I did look light to him, although I've never considered my hundred and sixty pounds as exactly scrawny. He was not only big; he was massive. An indifferently set broken nose gave his features a rakish but not a tough look. He seemed like a nice guy, although possibly not overly burdened with brains. We sat there talking football — rather, he talked and I listened. I needn't have worried about not knowing what to say.

The girl came back, looking in a somewhat better humor than before. We both stood up while Tom Pierce introduced me as an old football pal. Her name was Tony Caldwell.

I started to leave, but Tony slid into the booth and motioned me to sit beside her. "Sit down. You can talk football with Tom and get his mind off the lecture he's been giving me."

That sounded like good feminine logic. So far as I could tell she had been doing all the talking. Tom looked uncomfortable, but a dogged, determined expression covered the good humor on his face. "All I said was —" he began.

"I know what you said." She turned to me. "What about you, Mr. Marks? Would you take me to a night club if I asked you to?"

I would have, certainly, but it hardly seemed the thing to say at the moment. She wasn't really talking to me anyway.

"All I said —" Tom began again.

"Or would you want to ask my father first?" she demanded.

"All right, I'll take you." Tom gave in, but he wasn't happy about it. "Your old man will give me what-for, though, if he finds out. He doesn't want you to go to joints like the Arbor Club."

It seemed to me that her old man had good sense, but that again appeared hardly the thing to say. I said I was glad to have met them and started to leave, when they surprised me by urging that I go along with them.

I said that I didn't want to intrude. That wasn't entirely untrue — I was undecided as to the type of welcome my entrance into the Club Arbor might receive. Curiosity got the better of me, though, when they insisted. They were the oddest romantic twosome I ever saw.

"About this Arbor Club," I suggested as we drove along in the club coupé Tony had driven that afternoon, "are you sure that is where you want to go? I understand it is something of a dive."

"That's why I want to go," Tony said. "I'm tired of having Tom take me to places that he thinks will please Dad. Let him take dad if that's what he's interested in. Besides, I've met the manager of the Arbor and he's sort of cute. He said if I brought a party out I would be well taken care of."

The Arbor Club was less crowded than the previous evening, but was still filled to more than the capacity of its meager dance floor. While Pierce and I checked our hats, Tony looked around with frank interest. Then the bouncer spotted me and headed for us. He wore a long piece of sticking plaster running from his right eyebrow back along his head. The hair had been clipped under the bandage. He looked decidedly out of humor.

"You're askin' for it, bud," he growled at me, standing directly in front of us. His voice, high and almost squeaky, was not in keeping with the rest of his appearance. It didn't make him seem any less tough, though.

"You have the advantage of me," I said pleasantly. At least I tried to make it pleasant.

"You're not kidding there, bud. I can break you apart when I'm ready for you."

Tom Pierce smiled happily. "Take lots of time getting ready," he suggested. "You may find it turns into quite a chore." He was fully as large as the bouncer, considerably younger, and looked pleased at the sight of trouble. It was a comfort to have him there. "Let go my elbow, Tony. You can't say I'm starting this."

Tony didn't answer, but stepped directly between us and the bouncer and spoke to him. "You mustn't blame the boys for being so rude to you. You know how it is: they've had a little too much to drink. But I'll keep them quiet inside. Mr. Aims told me to come out and bring a party sometime."

The bouncer rubbed his ear reflectively, the initiative out of his hands. Tom's belligerence had disconcerted him; Tony had him entirely confused. I lit a cigarette and waited for developments. Then the man with the pinstripe suit of the night before, now wearing a loud affair of brown and green checks, was with us. A small lump showed through his thinning hair.

"What's the trouble?" he asked. "Why, Miss Caldwell, this is a pleasure."

He paid no attention to me, but he had seen me all right. "Hasn't anyone arranged for a table for you?"

"This man here was just promising to get us one," Tony said sweetly. "Mr. Walter Aims, this is Mr. Pierce and Mr. Marks."

We all shook hands. "You remind me of a man I used to know, Marks," Aims said gently.

"Must be coincidence. I'm a stranger in town."

"Well, any friend of Miss Caldwell's is a friend of mine. That's all, Joe," to the bouncer. "I'll find these people a table myself."

We went inside together, leaving Joe with a mystified expression. Things were moving entirely too fast for Joe's peace of mind.

Aims called a waiter and insisted that a table be set up on the edge of the floor for us. "A little floor show later on which I think you'll enjoy. I want you to have a good seat. Being Sunday, we only serve soft drinks." He winked at us and went away.

We settled down at the table. "Nice people you know," I said.

"Isn't he?" Tony asked gravely. "Really quite a fascinating man. I believe I want a Tom Collins."

Well, there are lots of things in the world I don't understand, but I try not to let that spoil my life. I had come along on a spur-of-the-moment impulse, because I was curious about the Colonel's change of attitude and was willing to spend a little spare time digging into the reason in spite of his sign-off orders. My curiosity would probably have been considerably less had not Tony Caldwell been a very pretty girl.

We danced a few times, although the floor was too crowded. I liked dancing with Tony. She lacked both the overwhelming affection and the icy rigidity displayed by Vera in her varying degrees of alcoholism. This girl drank very little, and with no apparent effect. Tom Pierce became just a bit louder and more friendly, but he didn't get drunk. They were both good company. I did not, however, get the slightest clue as to the Colonel's affairs.

I strolled into the wash room about twelve o'clock, when we were beginning to think of leaving. As I started out the door, it opened to admit Walter Aims. There was no one else in the room at the time. The window behind me was frosted glass, through which anyone outside couldn't possibly see anything but shadows. I put my back against a wall to eliminate even the chance of that shadow and nodded casually to Aims as he closed the door behind him.

"Nice place you got here," I said.

"Yeah, I like it." His voice was still urbane, though with none of the forced pleasantry he had shown earlier. It had a flat yet arrogant intonation.

"I wanted just a couple of words with you, Marks. Don't come around this place again. You've tied my hands tonight, seeing who you are with, but don't come around again. Guys don't pull what you did here and get away with it."

"Meaning just what for the future?" I asked evenly. I couldn't think of a better time or place for trouble between us if it was ever going to come. We were alone, and his back was against the one door, which opened inward. I was bigger and probably stronger than he was, and his hands were empty. Because I couldn't notice a gun on him didn't mean he didn't have one, but it meant he didn't have one in a very handy place. He wasn't apt to be so fast he could spot me an advantage like that and do me any harm.

"Meaning just don't come here. Nobody pushes me around twice in my own place."

"Your boys started things last night. I'm willing to let it drop there, if you are. But don't let me see any of your thugs around either me or the Colonel again, or we'll have real trouble. Is that plain on both sides?" I kept my voice carefully low and uncharged with any emotion.

"Plain enough. As far as I'm concerned last night was an accident — there'll be no repeat. But don't you come around here again."

"Now if that's settled, I'm about ready to leave. Any objections?"

"No objections." He stepped aside from the door and stood there watchin me.

"You first, please," I said, indicating the door. He locked eyes with me for a moment, then shrugged and went out. I followed and rejoined my table.

We left the Club shortly after that, driving around the city for a time, laughing and talking foolishness. It was all very pleasant. They dropped me at the hotel just after one-thirty. We all agreed to call up and arrange other parties, with none of us especially meaning it. It was just one of those sudden barroom friendships that are almost never followed up.

The night clerk told me the key wasn't in the box, so the Colonel appeared to be safely at home. I got in the elevator, run at this time of night by a muddy-complexioned female of indeterminate years. She took me directly to the eighth floor without a stop on the way, and without benefit of conversation. She looked about as disagreeable and uncommunicative as I figured I would be running an elevator at one-thirty in the morning. It was exactly twenty-five minutes to two when I left the elevator and rapped on the door to have the Colonel admit me.

There was no sound inside the room. I rapped again, louder, and finally banged on the door. The Colonel was ordinarily a light sleeper. I rang for the elevator.

"Please have the manager send up a pass key," I requested the operator. "Colonel Smallwood seems to have stepped out and forgotten to leave the key at the desk."

She looked at me with either suspicion or just plain dislike. "You want to ride down with me?" It was more a suggestion than a question.

"No, I'll wait here to see if he comes back. He might have just stepped into one of the other rooms on this floor."

That had a silly enough sound to it, but it served its purpose of sending her on her way. There wasn't any hurry, anyhow. If the Colonel had gone out he was probably all right — if he hadn't, that was something I didn't like to think about. I didn't care to leave the hall before seeing exactly what was inside that room, although that probably amounted to locking the barn after the horse was stolen.

The elevator came up again, empty except for the operator. She gave me a key. "You're supposed to leave it at the desk whenever you go out," she said. I thanked her and watched her close the door and start the car down.

When I unlocked the sitting room door, I found what I had been afraid of finding since my first tap on the door failed to elicit any response. The Colonel was seated in the armchair by the window, dressed as he had been during the afternoon. His attitude was natural enough except for the strained, twisted angle at which his head drooped forward. His right arm lay along the arm of the chair, and he was holding his little sleeve-gun in his gloved right hand. There was a powder-blackened hole in the front of his white shirt, just over the left breast, where the coat had fallen open. Even before feeling his wrist, I knew that the Colonel was dead, and had been dead for quite a while.

CHAPTER SIX

I CROSSED IMMEDIATELY to the telephone and got the night operator. "Room 807. There has been an accident. Will you have the manager come up immediately?" I hung up before she could say anything in return. I returned to the Colonel's body and slipped a key from the ring he carried at the end of his ornate gold watch chain, then went back to the desk and opened the brief case he had left there. There wasn't so much as a scrap of paper in the case. I had relocked the case and put the key back on the ring and in his pocket before the manager's knock sounded on the door.

The manager's reaction was not unnaturally one of fluttery excitement. Mr. Hawkins was a very ordinary sort of middle-aged man, in an ordinary sort of job, and this matter of finding a corpse in one of the chairs in his hotel upset him. With him was a big man, with a red, heavy-jowled face, thick curly hair and a perpetual scowl. He was smoking a cigar. All in all, he looked more like a movie version of a hotel detective than I would have believed possible, even including a rumpled and shiny-seated blue serge suit. He didn't introduce himself then, but I learned to know him later as Jack Cramer, the house dick.

He felt the Colonel's pulse, then scowled at me. "He's dead," he announced.

Hawkins made a sort of gargling noise in his throat. I was afraid for a moment that he was going to be sick on the rug. "He looked it to me," I agreed. "That's why I called you."

He went directly to the telephone and sent in a report to the police. I got out a bottle of the Colonel's scotch and put three glasses on the table. "Say when," I suggested to Hawkins.

"No . . . thanks, I don't believe I care for any. Thank you anyway." He sat down in a chair which faced away from the Colonel, then got up and stood awkwardly hesitant, plainly feeling that his position called for some action but not able to decide the proper course.

"How about you?" I asked Cramer, who had finished phoning.

"Put it away. No drinking now. I'll hear your story." His voice was the rough, intolerant rumble of a traffic cop bawling out a speeder.

I deliberately poured myself a small drink. "Whether you drink or not is up to you. And you'll hear my story when the cops get here, if they let you listen in." I tossed off the liquor.

He glared at me, but he let it go at that and began to wander about the room, peering intently at the furniture and other details which struck me as irrelevant. My reaction to him wasn't entirely due to irritation. I wanted a few minutes to fix things in my mind before the police came and possibly removed me from the scene. You can never tell how a cop will take to a private agency operative. The fact that the elevator operator knew I had gone into the room had made me afraid to delay calling the manager when I first got there.

The room was in perfect order — the maid must have done it up after I left. The Colonel was fully dressed and his suit was unrumpled. The chair he was in was the one he preferred to occupy. It looked like a perfect suicide set-up, even down to the fact that the gun in his hand was his own sleeve gun, except that the hand holding the derringer was wearing a glove. A plain, unlined leather driving glove which I hadn't seen before. A couple of cigar butts, the Colonel's brand, were in the ash trays. One used glass was beside his chair. Nowhere was there any indication of paper having been burned or destroyed, or any trace of another person having been in the room. I wandered into the bedroom, closely followed by Cramer, but found that also clean and bare in the impersonal way only a hotel bedroom can achieve.

I settled down on the davenport in the living room, thoughtfully drawing on my pipe. Cramer stared at me with hostility. "You take it calmly enough," he said. "Was you expecting him to knock himself off?"

I shrugged and didn't answer. Actually I was far from calm — was coldly furious, to say the least. The Colonel, so far as I had known him, was a fake, and as dishonest and immoral as he could get a chance to be. He was also a likable old scoundrel who had won a bit more of my affection than I realized until just then. And he was a client whom I had been hired to protect. Both personally and professionally his death was something which I felt. The suicide theory, so obvious to Cramer and Hawkins, was one that I just couldn't buy. The Colonel didn't fit my book as a man to shoot himself.

The city police were on the spot within an efficiently short time. A slight, gray-haired man neatly dressed in a gray business suit appeared to be in charge. He was accompanied by one morose-looking plainclothes cop, who appeared to be the fingerprint man, and several others in uniform, one of whom carried a camera. I had never happened to see a uniformed photographer before, but I found out later that this one didn't seem to be regarded as an oddity locally.

I stayed in the background while the gray-haired man talked briefly to the hotel men. He came over to me in a few minutes.

"I'm Sergeant Thomas. You found the body, I understand?" His voice

was that of an educated man, and was politely impersonal. Guessing his
occupation at another meeting, I would have picked him for a doctor or
lawyer.

"Yes, when I came home a few minutes ago. I had to send down to the
desk for the key."

"Your employer, was he?"

"Yes."

"Ever show any interest in suicide?"

I took my identification folder from my pocket and handed it to him.
"I don't think it's suicide, Sergeant. He was expecting something like this."

He looked carefully at the folder, then at me, satisfying himself that the
picture and I corresponded. "Watson Agency, eh?" he said thoughtfully.
He turned to the men who had come in with him. "Be especially careful,
boys. I'll want full pictures of everything. And check everything in the
place for prints. It may not be a suicide. What can you tell me so far,
Doctor?"

The heavy-set man who had been bending over the body straightened
up, surprise showing on his face. "Looks like a suicide to me. As nearly as
I can tell before the autopsy, he was shot with this weapon. It blew a hole
almost the size of a shotgun blast, but didn't go clear through him. Low
velocity weapon. He died instantly, or should have. He was shot close
enough for powder burns on the clothes. Been dead a couple of hours, at
least."

"Well, you may be right. But get on with it. Do you have a vacant room
on this floor, Mr. Hawkins?"

"The suite next to this is empty," Hawkins said nervously.

"Okay, we'll go in there in a minute." Sergeant Thomas prowled briefly
about the room, then the bedroom and the bath. "Just give me the key,
will you? I want to talk with Marks first. Will you and Cramer wait here
with the boys until I call you?" Then he said something to one of the uniformed cops, so low I couldn't catch the words, before turning to me.
"Will you step next door with me, Marks?"

I went with him, well enough pleased with the way he was going about it.

We settled ourselves in the living room of the vacant suite, which appeared to be a duplicate of the one we occupied. "Suppose you tell me
about it," he suggested.

I went over the entire story of my relationship with the Colonel from
the time he came to our office in New York, omitting nothing but my inspection of the brief case before the police arrived and Hart's crack about
San Francisco. There is no point in being too frank with any cop. He listened attentively, showing no evidence of incredulity but not letting me

see how he felt about it either. When I mentioned the name of Caldwell, he whistled softly and his eyebrows drew together in a slight frown.

"Why are you so sure he didn't kill himself? The position of the body is right for that. And it was his gun, wasn't it?"

"Yeah, it was his gun. I can't say exactly, aside from the fact that it doesn't fit in with the picture I have of the Colonel. I got to know the man pretty well, even in these two weeks. I don't think he meant to kill himself. The brief case might tell us something about that."

"It might." He looked at me speculatively. "I'll tell you what, Marks. You wait here a few minutes, and I'll go in and look around a bit. Where would the key to that case be, do you know?"

"On his key ring, I believe. Do you mind if I put in a call to my office while I wait?"

"Sure, go ahead. I'll be back."

When he left, I asked the operator to get New York for me. I knew that Thomas would have a man listening to that call, but I couldn't see that we had anything to hide. While I was disappointed that he apparently didn't intend to have me too close to him during the investigation, nothing could be done about that at the time. Trying to force myself in would do no good, and might damage the chance of his getting chummier in the future.

I was still alone in the vacant room, smoking and trying to get the picture really clear in my own mind, when my call from New York came through. The boss sounded mad, which was not too surprising at six o'clock in the morning, Eastern time. Still, the fact that he must have left instructions to put the call through to his home showed his interest in the case.

"What the hell?" he demanded. "Wouldn't it keep until breakfast?"

"Not too well. The Colonel was killed about an hour ago. At least I found him then."

"You found him?" I saw what he meant well enough. I wasn't supposed to find anything like that — I should have been there when it happened.

I sketched the details briefly. "He said the deal was off, whatever it was, and practically ordered me to leave him for the evening."

The chief's grunt was noncommittal but expressive. "Just how did you find him?" he asked.

I explained it to him. "It has the surface marks of a suicide," I said.

"Was it suicide?"

"I don't think so. Do we stay on the job?"

"We took his money, with the understanding that something like this might happen. Where are you calling from?"

"The hotel. The police made no objections." That should be plain enough warning to say nothing to me he didn't want overheard.

"Okay, you stay on the job, giving the police what help you can. Charley Sloan happened to be in Frisco finishing another assignment, so I have him checking that shooting scrape. He'll get in touch with you. Anything else you need?"

"I don't think so. I'll let you know if anything comes up." I was glad to hear that Sloan was already on the job in Frisco. I had a hunch that I might need all the leads I could get.

We hung up without further conversation. That was one thing about working for William Watson — if he trusted you, he gave you a free hand; if he didn't trust you, the job didn't last long. Of course, it was sometimes a matter of God help you if the results of that free hand weren't prompt and conclusive.

Sergeant Thomas came back in the room shortly after the call. He looked tired, but didn't have the mask of bad temper and hostility a lot of cops appear to feel is necessary to prove their minds are working on large problems. He sat down on the couch, stretched his feet out comfortably, and lit a pipe before he spoke. "Got your call through yet?" he inquired casually.

"Come now, Sergeant, we can be a little more frank with each other than that. I want to help out on this thing any way I can."

He grinned at me. "It wasn't much of a conversation," he admitted. "Nothing that helped me out, anyhow. Anything new occur to you?"

"Nothing so far. Any other questions you want to ask me?"

"Marks, I'll be frank. I want to clear this up, and until I have reason to suspect differently I'll assume you will help me all you can. We'll work together. Frankly, it looks like suicide to me. I wouldn't have much hesitation in writing it off as that, if you weren't so sure. Suppose you tell me again why it wasn't."

"First, the brief case. What was in that?"

"Nothing. I don't just mean nothing important, but nothing at all."

"What about the glove?"

"The mate to it was in the top drawer of his bureau in the bedroom. It doesn't look as though it has ever been worn, so the pair might have been Smallwood's and might not. Had you ever seen those gloves?"

"No, but that wouldn't necessarily mean he didn't own them — I didn't unpack for him. But why should a suicide put on a glove?"

He shrugged. "There are no rules on suicides, so far as I know. They do screwy stuff. Why shouldn't he?"

"I can think of better reasons for a murderer wearing the glove than a suicide. Tests would show whether the Colonel's hand was holding the weapon when it was fired — if the killer shot with a glove on and then put the glove on the dead man's hand, his fingers around the gun, so it would look like he fired it himself. Right?"

"Right," he agreed. "It could be. We're having the glove tested for powder marks. That old cannon should have left quite a backfire."

"When does the doctor think he was killed?"

"At least a couple of hours before we got here. He won't be more definite than that. The night clerk says Smallwood came down to the lobby about ten o'clock, put in a phone call from one of the booths that doesn't go through the switchboard, then went back to his room alone. At least the clerk thinks he was alone. We're sending a car for the elevator girl who quit at twelve o'clock. The girl on now says nobody except you came up to this floor or went down since she has been on duty."

"What does that prove? The killer could have used the stairs. In fact, if he was in his right mind, he undoubtedly used the stairs."

Thomas grinned sardonically. "Not these stairs. The doors lock automatically at eight o'clock and stay that way until seven in the morning. They are worked from a switch in the manager's office. Hawkins swears they were locked tonight, as usual. They're certainly locked now."

That staggered me. I never did care for these locked door mysteries. "What about somebody coming up earlier, and waiting behind one of those palms in the hall?"

"He could have come up and hidden," the sergeant agreed, "but what happened to him after that? I haven't seen him around anywhere."

"What about the other apartments?"

"It could be," he agreed again, "but frankly I don't believe it happened that way. I've looked at the list of the tenants of the other four apartments on this floor, and it doesn't seem probable that they are concerned. We'll interview them, of course. But I think he killed himself. Just what is your theory of who might have done it, Marks, leaving out the method for minute? Think it was Lucky Hart?"

"That doesn't seem too likely to me. Hart was out for the Colonel, sure, but mainly to collect the twenty grand that was lifted in that card game. I don't figure he would kill him without trying again to make him pay off."

"Was the game crooked?"

"I imagine it was, on both sides. Remember, I haven't tried to paint the Colonel as a Sunday School teacher. I think he was a card sharp by profession, and I had already wired the office to see whether the chief wanted to refund his money and pull me off the case. But this is murder, dammit, and I wasn't pulled off the case before it happened. That binds us to stick until it's cleared up."

"Was that affair at the Club Arbor connected with this, do you think?"

"I doubt it. They weren't trying to kill him. No weapons were showing, and it was too public. They just meant to rough him up. It could have been a tie-up with Lucky Hart, but I don't connect it with the killing."

"Don't you have any inkling of what he was scared of?"

"No. He was very close-mouthed on that, just like I told you. Frankly, I was beginning to wonder if it might not be some sort of blackmail. That was the only big deal I could see him making a killing on. And that would account for his fear of reprisal."

Thomas grinned ironically at me. "A nice spot for the Watson agency," he remarked. "I always heard of them as being on the up and up."

"They are. I've already told you I was getting set to pull out. But this visit to Caldwell's this afternoon was the first definite move he has made that would give me any indication he might be planning a shakedown. Even there, all I have to go on is that they were hardly the sort of people he would know."

"But you say that this afternoon the Colonel told you the deal was off, that he wouldn't need you. That sounds to me like whatever he may have planned fell through, so he came back here and shot himself. Doesn't it?"

"Knowing the old boy, it doesn't. He probably took a lot of knocks in his time, but I'll bet he always came up with another fool-proof scheme in his head. I could understand his killing somebody else, maybe, but not himself."

"It might be something in his past you don't understand. I'll check his army record — it might give us a line."

I laughed. "Five will get you ten that the army never heard of him. That title was as phony as the rest of him."

"You mix with nice people, Marks," the sergeant said flatly. "A lot of narrow-minded cops I know would get a little nosy about you trailing around with a man you figure to be a blackmailer, especially when he's been killed."

"I've told you how that was. And I wouldn't have told a lot of cops — I figure you really want to get this thing straight, and that is just what I want: to find who did the killing. I'll tell you anything I can to help that out. I don't hold with blackmail, and would have stopped it when I was certain, because he had no business dragging us into it, if that's what he did, but I hold with murder even less. Especially a man I'm supposed to look after."

"I see what you mean," he grinned. "It won't sound too well in the papers, will it? One of the boys on the squad says he has heard of you, and that you're supposed to rate pretty well in your own hangout. Who do you think the old man was trying to shake down?"

"I don't know," I said slowly. "But I figure we might know a lot more after a talk with Thornton Caldwell. And I'd like to know just where Caldwell was this evening."

Thomas looked at me for several minutes before he said anything. "Look, Marks, I'm willing to play along with you on this thing to any reasonable extent, although it still looks like an open and shut case of suicide to me. I'll go out and talk to Caldwell, to try to get a line on the Colonel's past — I'll even ask him politely if he was being blackmailed. I'll ask him if he knows why the old man should have committed suicide. Further than that I won't go, not until there is a lot more of an indication of murder here than I've seen so far. Caldwell is a big man in this town. Bigger maybe than you have any idea. I'm certainly not sticking my neck out on him like I might be willing to risk on Hart or Aims, for example, unless you can show me more to go on. Understand me: no man is above a murder charge. And if there is the slightest indication of that, I'll go for him in a minute. But some men are above being shoved around too much by detective sergeants, and as far as I'm concerned Caldwell is one of them. Get me?"

"You make it plain enough," I said. "Maybe it won't come to that. I have nothing definite to tie Caldwell in with the killing. What now?"

"On your theory, I believe we left your killer hiding behind the palms in the hall, after sneaking up the stairs before eight o'clock. Then he followed Smallwood in, heisted his gun, either took one of the old man's gloves or one of his own, in which case he hid the mate to it in the bureau, walked up close enough to leave powder burns on the shirt, and shot him. Then he put the glove on the dead man's hand, wrapped the fingers around the gun, and left. Incidentally, where did he go? Down the drain? Of course, we'll know more when we talk to the other elevator girl, but I can't see a killer advertising his visit that way."

"Are you sure the stairs are fool-proof? Could a block have been left in them before the automatic switch was pulled?"

"Impossible. If one of them isn't latched tight, a signal light shows downstairs."

"What about the fire escape at the end of the hall?"

"Window locked on the inside and hasn't been tampered with."

Thomas was talking completely seriously, yet I got the impression he was laughing at me at the same time. I didn't much blame him. On the face of it there appeared to be very little doubt of suicide, but it still didn't smell right to me. There had to be a way for the killer to have gotten in and out. The Colonel hadn't shot himself.

"How about the other people on this floor?" I asked wearily.

"Here is the list the manager gave me. I haven't talked to them yet. You can look it over, and then come along with me if you like. I don't want you to have any idea I'm trying to whitewash this thing."

I took the list, which contained only four sets of names. The hotel was a rather small one, tapering to almost a spire on this top floor, but I would still have imagined there were more than six sets of rooms. "Only six apartments here?" I asked.

"Yeah, they're all suites like this or larger. So that only leaves the four after your place and this vacant one."

The first name on the list was LeRoy P. Bronson, who had registered as being from Chicago. Then there was Mr. and Mrs. Henry Campbell, of Eugene, Oregon, a Major Edgar P. Harrison, and a Corporal Phillip Stevens. I tossed the paper back to Thomas.

"Expensive set-up for a corporal," he remarked.

"Corporals are people, just like anyone else," I told him, with an ex-enlisted man's touchiness on the subject. "If he has the money, why shouldn't he be as comfortable as the Major?"

He grinned at me. "I was in the 1918 affair myself," he said. "I know how you feel. Tell you what: if the Major has a woman with him, you can scare hell out of him if you want to. I've gotten to do it enough to sort of work that out of my system."

I felt a friendliness in him that hadn't been apparent before. He had evidently been an enlisted man himself, so that just talking about the Major made a bond between us.

"Okay, let's go. We'll try the officer and gentleman first."

We went out into the hall and knocked on a door. I noticed that our apartment door was still open, but that no one was around except a sleepy-looking uniformed cop sitting in a chair, where he had the entire hall in view. There was no answer immediately, so Thomas hammered again and harder.

"What is it?" a blurred voice sounded from inside.

"Police. Open up."

The door was opened by a short, tubby little man wearing a red striped bathrobe. His sparse hair was straggling down over his eyes; his pink, rather babyish face was twisted into a yawn. He certainly looked like a man who had just been awakened from a sound sleep.

We pushed our way past him. "I'm Sergeant Thomas, police," the sergeant told him, flashing his badge. "You're Major Harrison?" We went into the living room and sat down on the couch, the little man tailing after us.

"I'm Major Harrison," he agreed. "What's all this about?" He didn't sound too pleased, but under the circumstances it wasn't an unreasonable tone of voice.

"We just want to ask you a few questions. There's been an accident on this floor."

"Accident? What happened?" He looked confused, but certainly not alarmed.

"I'll ask the questions, Major." Thomas winked at me with the eye the Major couldn't see. "What time did you get in tonight?"

"I came up here directly after dinner at eight o'clock. I've stayed here all the time." The little man didn't sound exactly cowed, but he certainly wasn't giving us any excuse to get tough with him.

"Did you hear any unusual noises at any time?"

"No, I don't think so. Of course, my radio was on until about one, and these rooms are good about keeping out sound. What is all this about?"

"Do you know anyone in this hotel?"

"No, I just checked in yesterday. I have a ten day leave, and my wife is joining me here tomorrow."

"Does the name Smallwood mean anything to you? Colonel Alexander Smallwood?"

The Major rubbed his rumpled hair and thought for a while. "Not a thing. Never heard of the man. I only got back from overseas about a month ago, and don't know many people here. Is he in active service?"

"Not at the moment. Are you alone here, Major?" Without waiting for an answer, Thomas started to wander through the apartment. He was thorough, but didn't turn up anything.

"This is an outrage," the Major said rather tentatively. "I demand to know what this is all about." He seemed to feel that he should make more of a protest, but didn't exactly know how to go about it.

"Sure. We've had a suicide here, and just as a matter of routine we have to check through all the rooms on this floor. You can give me your outfit and station so I can verify what you've told me? Just routine."

"Certainly." The Major could understand routine, all right. He gave the address of a nearby camp. He was a quartermaster officer. "A suicide," he kept murmuring to himself. "Bless my soul."

"Okay, Major; sorry to bother you. Nothing else, except please don't leave town for a day or so without getting in touch with me. Anything you want to ask, Marks?"

"Nothing," I said. I couldn't feel strongly about the Major one way or the other.

Out in the hall, Thomas laughed softly. "You were mild enough," he observed. "Didn't he bring up the old feeling?"

"I've got other things on my mind. Whom do we see next?"

"Let's try Mr. and Mrs. Henry Campbell, in here. Not that I think anything will come of any of this." He knocked on the door, more moderately than when waking the Major.

Shortly we heard rustling sounds from within the apartment; then the door opened a small crack. "Yes?" a voice said.

"Police. May I talk with you for a moment?" Thomas sounded polite and unconcerned. He might have been delivering a telegram.

"Good God, police!" The voice sounded astonished.

"What is it, Henry?" This was a feminine quaver from an inner room.

The man at the door said: "It's the police."

There was a little scream from the bedroom. "Good heavens, what do they want?"

"I don't know," Henry told her.

"Let us in and we'll explain everything," Thomas suggested, without a ruffle in his calm. He seemed to be enjoying himself, in a quiet, undemonstrative sort of way.

The door opened wider and we walked in. Mr. Henry Campbell was an average sort of middle-aged man, now plainly bewildered and at something of a disadvantage because of the absence of his false teeth. Thomas introduced himself, and this time me as well, though only by name. Campbell excused himself to go into the bedroom. He came back in a moment or so with his teeth in his mouth and with a stringy-looking woman about his own age following him. Both were wrapped tightly in robes. She appeared to be in a state of pleasurable excitement.

"Goodness," she said, her voice high and rather squeaky, "I just don't know what to say about this. I've heard of such things, but it never happened to us before. I simply forgot to bring the marriage license with us this time, though I always try to have it with us on a trip."

"It is nothing like that, Mrs. Campbell," Thomas assured her gravely. "I'm Sergeant Thomas of the city police force. This is Mr. Marks. There happened to be an accident in this hotel tonight, and we hoped that you might be able to give us some information."

She may have looked a shade disappointed, but they both were interested in the word "accident."

"What happened?" she demanded.

"How long have you been in the apartment tonight?" Thomas evaded.

"Since before nine o'clock," she said hurriedly. Her husband was clearing his throat in an obvious prelude to speech, and she wanted to be the one to do the talking.

"Have you heard any unusual noises?"

"Nothing — nothing at all. We've been asleep since ten o'clock. At least I have — Henry reads until all hours of the night and probably didn't turn off his light until midnight. When did you turn off your light, Henry?"

"About midnight," Henry said dutifully. "I didn't hear anything."

The interview was not only uninteresting but entirely pointless. They had checked in at the hotel two days before, to visit their daughter taking summer courses at the University. Mr. Campbell was a hardware man in Eugene, Oregon. They didn't know any of the people at the hotel, although Mrs. Campbell had noticed the Colonel in the dining room and considered him a very distinguished-looking gentleman. Thomas made a vague excuse and searched through the apartment, but no one else was there. We left them thoroughly dissatisfied with the account given them of the "accident," but nevertheless pleasurably excited by the break in their routine. They certainly didn't have the appearance of a pair with anything on their consciences.

Out in the hall we saw a tall, blond young man in army uniform fumbling with the lock of the door to the next apartment. The uniformed cop was watching him from his chair against the wall.

"Corporal Stevens?" Thomas asked.

The soldier straightened up and looked hard at us, more from an effort to make his eyes focus than any real desire to see us. He was weaving slightly on his feet, but his voice was entirely clear and steady. "Yeah, that's me."

"May we see you for a few minutes?"

"Sure, anybody can see me. Especially if you can unlock this damn door. The keyhole bounces around."

I took the key from him and unlocked the door. We all went in. Corporal Stevens collapsed immediately into a large chair, waving an arm at us. "Sit down, make yourself at home. I don't know where we'll all sleep, but any pal of mine is welcome here. I've got one extra bed." He had given up trying to focus his eyes — just sat staring off into space. I felt a tinge of admiration for a man who could be that drunk and not show it more to the casual observer. He was almost out on his feet.

Thomas explained what we wanted and then looked around the rooms. No one was hiding anywhere in them. Stevens, watching with a vacant interest, said he had been out since five o'clock and couldn't remember where he had been except that it was bright and had lots of music and that he was almost broke.

"Still, have to enjoy all my furlough," he observed. "I'll wire my old man."

"What do you have against Colonel Smallwood?" Thomas asked suddenly, not really expecting any answer he could use.

"Just don't like him," the corporal said promptly.

"Where did you first meet him?"

"Never met him. But if he's a colonel, I don't like him. And if you're friends of his," the corporal said, looking stern, "I'm not sure you're friends of mine. What you doing here anyway?"

We took his organization and home address and left him snoring contentedly in the chair. "Pays all that money for a suite," Thomas grunted, "and sleeps in a chair. What do you think, Marks? Got any ideas yet where your murderer might have hidden?"

"Let's try the other room," I said. I was sleepy and disgusted and bothered by a growing certainty that, while I was sure the Colonel had not committed suicide, it was going to be awfully difficult to prove anything else.

The answer to our knock this time was quite a long while in coming. We heard no sound inside the rooms at all until the door opened suddenly to the limit allowed by the guard chain still kept on. We couldn't see the person opening it, but we heard a man's voice, low, guarded, neither sleepy nor surprised, say: "Who is it?"

"Police," Thomas said. "Open up, please."

"Cops, eh?" the voice said, somewhat louder, and the door was opened. LeRoy P. Bronson of Chicago stood blocking the entrance, looking at us with shrewd and suspicious little eyes. He was probably about forty years old, very much run to fat, a bright red dressing gown belted around him. "What you doing here?" He didn't sound friendly.

"Just taking a look around," Thomas said, pushing past him. The fat man gave ground reluctantly, but without physical protest, and we were all in the living room.

"Heck of a town," Bronson said bitterly. "Cops charging around at four o'clock in the morning. What you want?" His words were defiant but the tone was faintly uneasy.                                    ·

"You're Bronson?" Thomas asked. "I'm Sergeant Thomas. This is Mr. Marks. You alone in here?"

"Look, Chief," Bronson said, "you know how it is. I guess maybe there is a fine or something for this, but I don't want any publicity. Couldn't you take care of it for me? My home office is touchy about anything that gets in the papers."

"Well, well," Thomas said softly. "That's really interesting, Bronson. But this isn't a shakedown." He walked over to the bedroom door and opened it, emitting a low whistle when he looked inside. "Come out when you're ready," he said to someone in the room, and turned back to us.

Bronson had dropped into a chair, looking irritated but not exactly worried. "Chief, I'm travelling for Earnest and Company, out of Chicago. I've been in this town a lot of times and never had any trouble like this before. I'd rather not have any publicity, but I realize you boys have to make a living. We can settle this among ourselves all right."

"A murder is a tough thing to settle, Bronson. How high are you willing to go?"

The salesman sat up with a jerk. He looked shocked and frightened, but perhaps not unduly so under the circumstances. "What in God's name you talking about?"

A girl came out of the bedroom then, a tall, very thin girl of perhaps twenty-two. Her long blonde hair was the peroxide type, and she had taken time to smear lipstick on her wide mouth. She was wearing a flimsy wrap-around robe.

"A raid, huh?" she said casually. Her voice had a rough, throaty quality that might have been caused by too many cigarettes. She sauntered over and sat down on the couch beside me. "How about a cigarette, copper?"

I gave her one and struck a match for her. Then I pulled out my pipe and lit it, while Bronson sat there breathing heavily and Thomas allowed the silence to drag on. The blonde straightened the robe around her and leaned back, drawing on her cigarette and apparently unconcerned.

"You boys are new around here, aren't you?" she said finally.

"We're not the vice squad," Thomas told her. "We're homicide." If he expected a reaction from that, he was disappointed, except for a sort of anguished grunt from Bronson. The girl raised her eyebrows and said nothing at all.

"What's your name?" Thomas snapped at her. "And your address?"

"Eleanor La Tour," she told him. And she named an address.

"Want to tell us about it?"

"There's nothing to tell," she said, smiling faintly. "Nothing you can't see for yourself. Even homicide must get around enough to figure this out."

Thomas stood up abruptly. "If that's the way you want it, okay. Get your clothes on. We're taking you in. Maybe you'll talk more when you see Aims' written confession."

That jarred everyone into action, and gave me some surprise myself. I couldn't follow the sudden change of front at all. Bronson came to his feet, squawking like a chicken. The girl ground out her cigarette and stared at Thomas, her eyes and mouth hard.

"You can't do that," Bronson protested. "I don't know anything about any murder — I haven't even been out of this hotel since eight o'clock. She came about nine-thirty and we've been together since then. We can both swear to it. Listen to reason, Chief. You got no evidence to haul us in."

The girl didn't say anything.

Thomas looked speculatively at the fat man. "Don't try to pull that innocent act. Aims talked, I tell you. Get your clothes on."

"Wait a minute," I said, beginning to catch the drift. "The girl and Aims may have just played him for a sucker. He may not know what she did when she went out. He might be on the level."

"I don't know what you're talking about," Bronson moaned. "Neither of us has been out of the room, not since nine-thirty. What happened around here, anyhow?"

"It's a bluff of some kind," the girl told him. "He pulled that right after I told him my address. That's when he brought Aims into it. Try again, copper. I don't know what all this is about, but I doubt if Aims talked about anything."

I sat back and watched while Thomas went round and round with them. As far as I could tell, they weren't holding out anything. Bronson, especially, didn't look like a hard man to break down, and he seemed genuinely confused. The girl might be a different matter, but I was inclined to believe the salesman when he swore that neither of them had left the room since nine-thirty and that the blonde was just a girl from a house who had been sent up by arrangement with Jack Cramer. That fitted in with my opinion of Cramer, all right.

The implications concerning Aims gave me more food for thought. He was apparently more than a night club operator around town. I hadn't figured him for a hand in the killing, but it was quite a coincidence that a girl from his house, or one of his houses, was spending the night in a room on the same floor. Still, I had a feeling that Bronson would prove to be the salesman he claimed, out for an evening's fun, and he swore the girl wasn't out of the room.

Thomas got little else from them, although I gave him credit for being as skillfull at questioning as any cop I ever saw. He was alternately tough and beguiling, threatening and friendly. He could probably have gotten anything that he wanted from the fat salesman, if the salesman had known it. The girl was faintly restless and uneasy beneath her hard exterior, but she wasn't talking. Finally she stood up angrily.

"Break it up," she said harshly. "We're in the clear on this thing, whatever it is. You've no right to be here at all — we don't know anything about it. Get out."

"If that's the way you want to be, okay," Thomas said softly. "We'll continue this at the station."

"You don't have anything on us," she said furiously.

"A state vagrancy charge should hold you nicely until something else comes along. That can be just about what we want to make it — you should know that."

She did know it, obviously, and for the first time she looked scared. "Walter Aims will take care of that for us. And he'll take care of you, too, copper," she said, but her heart wasn't in it. She was worried.

"Some cops in this town may have their hands out for easy money," Thomas said, with the first real anger I had ever heard him express, "but you are going to find a murder damned hard to square. If you're smart, you won't try to tell me what Aims or anyone else will do to me about that."

She knew it was true, and changed her attitude. "Sergeant, I swear this is just what we say it is. Cramer phoned for a girl for this room and I came up. I don't know a thing about what went on anywhere else, and I'm sure Mr. Bronson doesn't either. Give us a break — it can make a lot of trouble for me if they book me again. We can't get away, and I'll help you any way I can. I might hear something."

Bronson added his vehement plea. Thomas finally let them alone, with warnings to keep in touch with him. Out in the hall, he looked at me, a bit shamefaced.

"Probably I should have run them in, but I haven't time to fool with it now. Not till we get more to go on. And what good does it do to make it tough for one girl?"

We returned to the room the Colonel and I had occupied together. It was now nearly five in the morning. Thomas told the fat cop to go on home and get some sleep, an offer which he accepted promptly. Then we sat there looking at each other.

"I can't see it, Marks," he finally said. "It looks like suicide from every angle to me. I'll check on the information these other tenants gave me, of course, and I'll see Aims and Lucky Hart, if he is still in town, but it looks like suicide to me."

I was too sleepy to argue, and it wouldn't have done any good anyhow. Thomas was a good cop; he was going through all the motions I could have asked of him. It was unreasonable to expect him to agree with me in the bargain. "Tell me about Aims," I suggested.

"There's nothing much to tell that you haven't seen or heard. He's not too big a noise around town, but he has something of an in with the right people. He runs the Club Arbor and a couple of bars, and operates a couple of houses. The way I hear it, he just plays ball and doesn't make any trouble, so no one makes trouble for him."

"You don't think the Colonel might have had some kind of shakedown scheme on hand with him, then?"

"It's possible. He could get his hands on quite a bit of dough if he had to, probably. The thing is, what would you blackmail him about? It would have to be a killing or a Federal rap or something of that sort to bother him — he wouldn't give a hoot for publicity. And he has been operating around here for fifteen years or so. I would expect to hear a hint of anything like that. When the girl gave an address I recognized as one of Aims' houses, I tried to blast an admission out of her or the salesman, but I didn't have too much faith in it. My guess is that they were telling the truth."

A uniformed cop came in then, looking tired and walking as though his feet hurt him. "I've talked to the elevator girl, Sarge. She kicked about coming down here this time of night, and you said not to push it if she didn't know anything."   ·

"Did she know anything?"

"Naw. She said the only time she saw the old gent was when he came down to the lobby for a few minutes, a couple of hours before she went off duty. She didn't notice the time particularly. He rode back up to the eighth floor by himself. She didn't take anybody else up there either then or later."

The sergeant asked him if the girl had noticed anything unusual about the Colonel when he made his trip down to the lobby. The cop grinned a little at this. "She said the only thing she noticed was that he didn't try to pat her, like he usually did."

Thomas and I looked at each other. "I still say it wasn't suicide," I insisted stubbornly. "What's your next move?"

"Bed," the sergeant said promptly. "I'll start the wires moving on a few of these items and then get some sleep. How about you?"

"Sounds okay. I never quite swallowed these storybook detectives who get along by swapping liquor for sleep. Where do we stand — are there any strings on my movements?"

"No strings at all, Marks, though we might sort of keep an eye on you. I take it you are going to be around here for a time?"

"That's right. I won't be leaving town."

He shook hands with me and left, after suggesting that I meet him at the downtown station at noon the next day to go with him when he talked to the Caldwells. I agreed readily enough.

CHAPTER SEVEN

I DIDN'T WAKE up until nearly eleven o'clock Monday morning. I yawned, sat up in bed, and had almost taken the telephone off the hook to order breakfast before I remembered that from here on my expense account would go in to Watson and Company instead of being taken care of by the Colonel. The chief wasn't much of a believer in his men having breakfast in bed, so I began to dress. I looked around the suite of rooms and decided that I could probably justify their expense for a few days more by pleading the necessity for remaining at the scene of the crime. That made me feel better — I liked it there.

The morning elevator girl gave me the attention due a man coming out of a room in which a dead body had been found. I thought for a moment that she might ask for my autograph.

Jerry the bellhop met me in the lobby. With an elaborately conspiratory jerk of his head he beckoned me into a more or less secluded corner. Without wasting time on preliminaries, he put his proposition — for one hundred dollars, cash, he would give me an alibi, guaranteed iron-clad for any time I chose.

Having always prided myself on a knowledge of my own limitations, I wasted no time trying to reform that kid. I just told him that I had an alibi.

Seeing the speculation come suddenly into his eyes, I added: "And don't get any blackmailing ideas. It happens not to be a fake. I'm an innocent man."

I couldn't quite classify the look on his face as I went into the coffee shop, but it could have been admiration. Certainly it wasn't belief. The word "innocent" wasn't in that kid's vocabulary.

I had a cup of coffee and started for my appointment with Sergeant Thomas. Catching a bus at the hotel door, I estimated that the expense account could easily bear a dollar charge for taxi fare.

The city hall was one of the oldest and dirtiest buildings I have ever seen in a fairly long career in and around civic buildings. Its dark halls wandered off into a rabbit warren effect, and finding your way to any particular spot appeared hopeless. With the office space like that, it didn't take much imagination to picture the jail. I made a mental note to avoid irritating Sergeant Thomas too much, since the idea of spending even one night in the place had no appeal.

The cop on the desk directed me to the homicide offices. No one was in the waiting room, but I stuck my head in the first open door to find Thomas sitting at a battered desk, thumbing distastefully through a small stack of papers. A colorless, stringy woman on the wrong side of forty was looking through a filing cabinet.

Thomas gave me a faint grin, holding just a hint of derision. "Hello, Marks. Have a chair."

The woman looked up immediately. She gave a small sigh and stared at me, as though she wanted to memorize every detail. My usual effect on her sex was something less than that, ranging all the way from complete indifference to possibly a faint interest. In the latter event they were generally sitting alone in some bar.

"The private detective?" she asked in a breathless sort of voice. "The one who is going to solve the Smallwood case for you?"

Sergeant Thomas, in an "I give up" sort of voice, said: "Miss Jensen, Mr. Marks."

She crossed the room and held out her hand, keeping her eyes fixed on mine. I shook hands with her. "I am glad to meet you," she said, under-lining the "am." The whole thing struck me as about as pointless a gag as I ever ran across.

"Miss Jensen reads," Thomas explained, clearing it up. "She reads detective stories, before, during and after office hours. She has completely absorbed their lesson that all cops are either fools or crooks or both, and that all private agency men are knights in shining armor." Miss Jensen looked a bit embarrassed, but she didn't deny it. "Twenty years she has worked in this department, ten years she has worked for me. And still she is convinced that every killing which looks like a suicide is really murder, and vice versa. I tell you, Miss Jensen, this Smallwood character actually did commit suicide."

Her bony jaw set stubbornly. "I'm sure Mr. Marks doesn't agree," she said. "Perry Mason —"

"Damn Perry Mason," Thomas almost yelled. "Damn Mr. Marks. Get those letters out."

She left the room with dignity, not at all discomposed. "We'll be glad to help you any way we can," she assured me as she passed.

Thomas and I looked at each other in silence for a time. I was glad when he started to laugh — I couldn't have held out much longer without breaking down myself.

"Well, damn it, it does get on my nerves sometimes. She means every word of it, too. Anyhow, I'm afraid she's wrong this time, Marks. I've had the boys doing some checking. There's nothing to indicate that those people on the eighth floor had any reason either to do the job themselves or help someone else do it.

"There's no other way it could have been done, what with the locked stairway doors and the unused elevator. We can even rule out the idea of someone else hiding in the other apartments — he would have had no chance to get down before we searched the place. So either it is suicide, or one of those five people killed him — Bronson, his blonde girl friend, the army Major, or one of the Campbells. The corporal came back after we were there, so that lets him out.

"I've checked on the others pretty well. Major Harrison is just what he says he is. Before going in the army in '39, he was a mail carrier in Kansas City. No sign of any homicidal tendencies or gangster connections.

"The Campbells check out — he's a hardware man on a visit to his daughter. Not a sign of a connection there.

"Bronson is a Chicago travelling man. Here is the telegram his firm sent in answer to my wire."

He tossed me a sheet of paper. It said: "LeRoy P. Bronson represents this firm during business hours stop reasonably honest during business hours stop now staying Essex Hotel your city supposed to be alone but probably is not stop we will back him up if he is in a jam but do not tell him I said so stop." It was signed by Walter Hazel, sales manager.

"Sent collect," Thomas explained. "It's easy to be funny on someone else's money. But they seem to be sure enough that he wouldn't get mixed into anything serious.

"That brings up the La Tour girl. She sounds more reasonable on the face of it, of course, but there's really nothing to go on with her. She's well known to the vice squad. Just an ordinary prostitute, never especially connected with Aims except that she works in one of his houses. She's been there a year — been active in the racket here nearly four years, since she finished high school. And Bronson backs up her story that she never left the room. If he wasn't telling the truth, he's a better liar than the average."

I agreed with him there. In addition, it just didn't seem reasonable that Lucky Hart or Aims would have handled the killing that way — through a girl whose connection could be traced back to them.

"Oh, yes, and there were powder marks on that glove. It held the gun all right. And the other glove was in one of the dead man's bureau drawers. Even if we lined up a motive, Marks, what jury would ever convict with that kind of set-up?"

"What about this Caldwell?" I asked.

"Caldwell is a very big man, as I told you. He owns a steamship line and a couple of lumber companies."

"Politician?"

"Yes and no. He is the not-so-secret big gun in the battle industry is making against the unions around here just now. He swings a lot of weight — why would he want to kill a tin-horn gambler?"

"I've been reading something about that battle," I said. "They're out to discredit the union bosses, aren't they? Raking up criminal records and that sort of thing?"

"That's right."

"He would be a nice blackmail target, wouldn't he?" I asked conversationally. "And probably not the kind of man to take it lying down."

Thomas laughed. "So the old boy was blackmailing Caldwell and gets knocked off, eh? Possibly, Marks, but we get right back to how it was done. Caldwell is a powerful man, but I never heard that he could go through locked doors. No, it looks like suicide to me, and that's the way I've given it to the papers. Meantime I'll put LaTour and Bronson through it again, but unless we get a break out of them it just couldn't have been anything else. And I have other things to do — I can't spend too much time on an open and shut deal like this."

I didn't argue with him. For one thing, it would have done me no good. His mind was entirely made up, and I could see his point of view. Suicide was the reasonable solution, certainly more of a desirable one to the department than an unsolved, impossible murder. Still, I was irritated. Last night I had expected to find him willing to go a bit further into the matter. He had promised to grill Caldwell, but obviously one of his superiors had changed his mind.

I stood up and said politely: "You'll be interested if I get a confession?"

He wasn't sore. "Don't be like that, Marks. You give me a shadow of evidence to go on, and I'll follow it up with you. I just can't see sticking my neck out, annoying Caldwell, with a fishing expedition. I take it you're going to see him. That's all right with me, but leave me out of it."

That was fair enough, really. He wasn't trying to throw anything in my way, when he could have thrown plenty. I told him I appreciated that and went out into the outer office.

Miss Jensen looked up eagerly. "Mr. Marks," she said, "I read one time of a case where they unlocked a doorway with a pin and a piece of string. Do you suppose those stair doors —?"

"Steel fireproof doors?" Thomas inquired politely over my shoulder. "And with automatic locks?"

I thanked her and said I would certainly look into that angle.

CHAPTER EIGHT

I GAVE THE cab driver a two-bit tip, turned my back on his slight sneer, and started up the curving walk to the Caldwell mansion. It was a bright day, but the sun didn't warm my back when I thought of the Colonel marching up this same walk to pay the last visit he ever made.

Before I had a chance to lift the ornate bronze knocker, the door was opened. There stood the butler, bending that nasty, drill sergeant expression right at me.

"Still sightseeing?" he asked.

I didn't care for his tone, but decided to play it straight. Without comment, I handed him an agency card. He looked it over and didn't appear impressed.

"What do you want?" he asked. He didn't quite say "youse" but he came close.

"I want to see Mr. Caldwell."

"What about?"

I still didn't care for the tone, and enough is enough. I put an edge to my own voice to say: "I'll have to take that up with him. Just announce me, please."

He grunted and stepped back. Accepting that as some sort of invitation, I pushed the door wider and went in. We stood there in the spacious tile-floored entrance hall, measuring each other with our eyes for a good ten seconds.

"Wait a minute," he said grudgingly. "I'll speak to the boss."

He went up a broad staircase, leaving me standing there, staring at his back. I felt that it would be a pleasure to have an excuse to slug him, though it might very well be costly. He was a well-put-together lad, walking lightly on the balls of his feet and keeping himself on balance all the time. The right-hand pocket of his sack coat sagged noticeably.

The only room I could observe from the chair I helped myself to was set down perhaps a foot below the level of the hall. I could see about fifteen feet of one end of it, including an entire panel of glass that looked out over the bay. It was a luxurious room, with heavy, deep chairs, squat tables, and a great semi-circular couch curving before the picture window. It must have cost plenty, and I sat there trying to figure out why anyone with all that money didn't blow himself to a butler with better manners.

The drill sergeant would have been more at home patrolling the grounds outside with a tommy gun under his arm.

Two women came into the room while I watched. They sat down on the couch, which was at an angle partly beyond my vision, so that only their legs were visible. Well, that was better than nothing. I like something to look at while I'm waiting. I recalled the time Charley Sloan and I had been staked out behind the swinging doors of the men's room of an East Side bar, waiting for Luigi, the owner, to put the finger on a guy for us. We were there three nights, with nothing much to do but watch passing legs and bet on the women's ages. Sometimes when we couldn't agree we would put up real money and send Luigi to find out for us. We both got pretty good, but Charley was ten dollars ahead before I found out Luigi was selling me out and splitting the pot with him.

Anyhow, judging these legs now on display, I figured the bare ones on the side nearest me to be about twenty. They were long and smoothly tanned, and could have belonged to Tony Caldwell. The other pair, encased in stockings, were almost as trim, and a man without that three days' experience might have guessed them to be the same age. Not the old master, though. I would have bet a dollar cash that their owner would never see forty again.

Either the two women were talking very softly or the big room muffled the sound, because their voices were faint and indistinct. I was none too anxious to see Tony Caldwell just then and so sat quietly. That was, of course, the time I had to pick to sneeze, loudly and violently.

The bare legs got up and walked over to the bottom of the steps. They belonged to Tony, all right. She smiled at me, though possibly with some astonishment.

"This is nice," she said. "How are you?" She came up the step from the big room and held out her hand, so I shook it. She had long, cool fingers and a grip that was firm without being masculine. I was sorry to be there on business.

I took a card out of my pocket and handed it to her, watching her face as she glanced at it. You often have to be a heel in my business. I didn't get any dividends from it this time, though. She started to laugh when she read the card, and so far as I could tell, there was no trace of either alarm or shock.

"Don't tell me you were on business last night?" she asked. "I thought your interest in football was a shade overdone. Is Tom going to be a divorce correspondent?"

"I'm not a divorce detective," I told her. "I haven't peeked over a hotel room transom in years."

"Who is it, Tony?" The other woman had crossed the big room, and I surveyed her over the girl's shoulder.

She was forty, all right, and probably a number of years beyond, but well-preserved and put together. She was tall, quite slender, with an abundance of reddish-brown hair showing a few faint streaks of gray. My first impression was that she was a most attractive woman — my second, that she was either a very worried or unhappy woman, or both.

"Mother, this is Jonathan Marks. He is a detective. He came here to —" She turned to me. "Just why are you here, Jonny? I take it from the card that you aren't paying a purely social call." Her voice was light and amused — it was impossible to read any hidden meaning or anxiety into it.

My attention, however, was only partly held by Tony's voice. The effect of her words on the older woman was pronounced. Her eyes widened in some emotion, gone too quickly for me to attempt to classify, before she took hold of herself and smiled pleasantly.

"How do you do, Mr. Marks?" she said, her voice under perfect control. "That was a rude question, Tony. I'm sure Mr. Marks will tell you what he wants in good time. Won't you come in?"

It was well done — so well that I wondered if that startled expression had been only my imagination. "Thanks," I said, "but I'm hoping to see Mr. Caldwell."

"Dad's upstairs. Does he know you're here?"

"Your butler went to tell him, I believe."

"Excuse me," Mrs. Caldwell said. "I'll go and remind him myself." She smiled impersonally at me and started upstairs.

"Come on in," Tony suggested. "Briggs shouldn't have kept you waiting out here in the hall."

"I don't think Briggs likes me very well," I told her as I followed her into the big room.

She motioned for me to sit on the sofa where she and her mother had been talking, and sat down beside me. "Probably not," she agreed. "He doesn't seem to like anyone but Dad. He is a sort of bodyguard, too. Dad thinks the revolution is just around the corner. Have a drink?"

I declined the drink. She made even Briggs sound plausible and unimportant. She was as attractive as the very devil. I was sorry that she wasn't a waitress I had picked up for the evening, rather than an heiress I might be interested in professionally.

"Then tell me all about the detective business," she urged. "I suppose it wouldn't do any good to try and find out why you're here, so tell me about something else."

I told her about Luigi and the three-day wait in his bar. She seemed interested. She stretched her legs out in front of her and surveyed them critically. "Will you really be able to tell the difference in them in ten years?" she asked anxiously.

A cough interrupted us, and there stood Briggs, the butler, looking like a particularly murderous old maid aunt. "Mr. Caldwell will see you now," he said. "Sir," he added, as though the word pained him a good deal.

Tony got up and walked to the window, keeping her back to us. Her shoulders were shaking. "Stop in to see me when you leave," she suggested, her voice choking with laughter. Briggs gave me a look that told me it would be over his dead body. The sagging weight in his pocket kept me from fully appreciating the humorous aspects of the situation.

He led me into an upstairs room which was a masculine, leather-finished reproduction of the one downstairs. There was a big desk in a corner by one of the windows. A tall man wearing a brown business suit which hadn't been pressed recently got up from a chair by the desk and stepped forward. He was about the Colonel's age, lean, his face deeply lined under sparse gray hair. The mouth was thin-lipped, tight at the corners. Altogether he looked to me to be another lad who in his own way could be as tough as necessary.

When he spoke, however, his voice was clipped and precise but not unfriendly. "Mr. Marks?" he said. "I'm Thornton Caldwell." He shook hands with me, a quick, firm grip. "And this is Mr. Hansen, a business associate." The other man in the room also shook hands.

Hansen was a curly-haired, good-looking fellow of about thirty-five. His gray flannel suit was well-cut and immaculately pressed. Although almost a collar ad in appearance, he didn't seem entirely the pretty boy type. There was a pugnacious rake to his jaw, and his eyes were as hard and veiled as any I have ever looked into. I had little hope of getting any information which these two didn't want to give away. Still, as long as a man will talk, he is apt to let something slip.

"Have a chair, Mr. Marks," Caldwell told me, indicating one which looked and proved to be very comfortable. "What can I do for you?" Then, noticing the butler still hovering near the door: "That's all, Briggs. I won't need you."

"The guy's got a gun on him, Chief. I just tumbled to it. Shoulder holster."

Caldwell surveyed me, a hint of a smile twisting the corners of his mouth. "Has he, indeed? His clothing certainly hides it well — I would never have guessed. But Mr. Marks is a detective, Briggs, and probably has every reason to carry a gun. You may go now."

Briggs went, but he wasn't happy about it. Caldwell and Hansen both laughed as the door closed behind him. "That boy takes his bodyguard job too seriously," Hansen commented. His voice had a pleasant intonation which I placed as the product of some New England University.

Caldwell shrugged. "He means well, and I feel safer having him around when the women are here alone. Some of those fellows would stop at nothing. And now, Mr. Marks?"

"This is a rather confidential matter," I suggested. "Would it be convenient for me to see you alone?"

"I'm sure that won't be necessary," he said definitely. "Mr. Hansen is more than a mere business associate. He is actually my confidential secretary. I have no secrets from him. I would prefer to have him stay."

"I wanted to ask you a few questions about Colonel Smallwood, Colonel Alexander Smallwood."

"Oh, yes, the man who was here yesterday. Certainly, although I know very little about him."

Hansen leaned forward suddenly. "He's dead, Mr. Caldwell. Suicide at the Essex Hotel. I heard it over the radio before I came. Meant to tell you."

If it was an act, it was well done. Hansen looked at me with just the right touch of suspicion for trying to pump Caldwell without giving him full information. Caldwell himself looked surprised but not unduly shocked — more or less as you might expect a man to react on hearing of the death of a casual acquaintance.

"Suicide," he murmured. "Extraordinary. He scarcely seemed the type."

"You never know about that," I said. "Our trouble is that we don't have much information about him. I hoped you might tell me something more."

"Almost nothing, I'm afraid. I never saw him before yesterday. He called me up in the morning, mentioned the name of an Eastern associate of mine, said he wanted to discuss investments. I told him to come along. He turned out to be just another oil stock salesman, with a not-too-good proposition. I doubt that he even knew Dalton, the man to whom he referred."

"Did he stay long?"

"Quite a while — he had a good line and he amused me. But you should know how long he stayed. Briggs tells me you were taking an interest in the matter." This was said casually, without apparent malice or annoyance.

"Did he show you any stock certificates, a prospectus, anything in writing?"

Caldwell either avoided the trap or was innocent of any knowledge of it, for he thought a moment and said: "No, he just talked. With a silver tongue, I might add. Isn't that your recollection, Pete? Mr. Hansen was with us," he explained to me. Hansen said that was about the way he remembered it.

It sounded quite convincing. Oil stock was a real possibility with the Colonel, and Caldwell had described his actions just as they would have been. He hadn't seen anything in writing, which did not disagree with the fact that nothing of the sort was found among the Colonel's effects, nor with my observation that he had apparently taken nothing with him when he called on Caldwell.

Thornton Caldwell, however, had told one smashing lie. The Colonel had not telephoned him or anyone else before that Sunday visit — I had been with him without exception during the entire time.

I left fifteen minutes later without anything much to add to that one disclosure. They were both politely impersonal, willing to be helpful but with just a trace of a "this is really no concern of mine" attitude. That was natural and unsuspicious, if Caldwell's relations with the Colonel were as he represented them. One thing only did not quite ring true — neither of the men displayed the slightest curiosity as to why a private investigator should be interesting himself in a matter in which the police had made no move. They acted as though it were an entirely natural circumstance.

"Pete, show Mr. Marks to the door," Caldwell said.

The heavy carpet on the stairs made my descent noiseless, so that I got a good look at Briggs before he saw me. He was standing in the hallway with his back toward me. A tray with a cocktail shaker and four glasses was on a table beside him. I watched him drain a fifth glass, wipe the inside with a handkerchief, and replace it on the tray.

"That's not hygienic," I told him from the foot of the stairs.

He turned around slowly and surveyed me, making no secret of his unflattering opinion. "If that means it ain't healthy," he said, "I could tell you things that are more so. Here's your hat, pal. Miss Caldwell isn't seeing you." He picked up my hat from the chair on which I had left it and handed it, practically threw it, to me. Then he turned to open the door.

Acting on impulse, I scooped up the glass he had just placed on the table and slid it into my coat pocket, holding the hat carelessly in front of the bulge. The guy must have had eyes in the back of his head. As I walked past him, his elbow jerked sharply, smashing into the top of my hat hard enough to let me feel a solid smash against my side. There was a crunching sound as the cocktail glass splintered in my pocket.

"Sorry, pal," he told me, dead pan. "My foot slipped. You got to watch that around here — be careful yours doesn't."

To say that I returned to the hotel in a disagreeable frame of mind was putting it mildly.

It was then three o'clock in the afternoon. I sat for a time, sorting the pieces of the puzzle over in my mind. That didn't take long, because there weren't many pieces apparent to me as yet. Becoming discouraged with the results of purely mental activity, I decided to try something else.

CHAPTER NINE

I WENT OVER to the phone and put in a call for the manager. I asked him to send Jack Cramer, the house dick, up right away. Hawkins' voice dripped with curiosity as he asked if there was anything he could do himself, but he promised to have Cramer there in five minutes.

Cramer came in truculently, his hard, piggish little eyes boring at me. "You find another body?" he asked.

It was actually a relief to talk to Cramer. I was mad, frustrated, and I had been made to look like a fool on several embarrassingly recent occasions. At a time like that there is a childish satisfaction in letting your irritation boil over on someone, and this looked like the right spot.

"Sit down," I snapped at him. "I want to talk to you."

He was somewhat less than intimidated. He took a step toward me and snarled: "Who you think you're talking to? I got a notion to slap your ears down for you." He looked as though he meant it.

"I'm talking to an article I've got small use for, and that's a badge-wearing pimp. Sit down. Make a pass at me and I'll lay you out. Then I'll have a talk with the hotel management about your little sideline, about the women you bring here."

The first part of the threat didn't bother him — he could probably have taken me handily — but the last sentence stopped him in his tracks. He blinked at me a couple of times.

"Or maybe you would like to have me talk to them about the blackmail angle. I said sit down!"

This last was purely a shot in the dark, based on a not too difficult appraisal of the man's character. He sat down abruptly, the threatening look entirely gone.

"What you sore at me about, Marks?"

Well, enough is enough. I felt better, and there was no need for carrying things on in such a strident manner. He had seen the threat, acknowledged its effect, and there was more to be gained by handling him smoothly, not driving him to a point where his own anger and self-respect would hold him to a course he was willing enough to drop. Even Cramer probably had something he called self-respect.

"Sore at you?" I asked, trying to sound surprised, and taking the edge from my tone. "I'm not sore. I just want you to quit pushing me around and cooperate with me. Have a drink?"

"Yeah, thanks." He looked intensely relieved while I poured him a generous slug of the Colonel's Scotch, taking one for myself that I didn't really
want. "You got me wrong, Marks. I'd like to work with you. I figure we
could show these city cops a thing or two."

"I want to know about the La Tour girl — all about her."

"Honest to God, there isn't much to know. Bronson talked to me — he's
been here before — about a girl. Just to help him out I called this house.
Some guy had told me about it, I forget who. They must have sent La
Tour. I never even saw her. I never got a nickel out of it, naturally. I
wouldn't touch that kind of dough. Just being a good guy."

"Sure," I said, letting the tone harden a bit, "but I want more than that.
Who is she? Where is she from? Who are her friends?"

He took the hint. "Well, I do happen to know something about her. She's
all right, I think. Lived with her folks out on the north side all her life. The
old man was a clerk down at the city hall, name of Smith. Mother dead
for years. Smith died several years ago, and she sort of drifted into the
racket."

"Did you ask for her especially?"

"No, I just told them to send up a blonde, and gave them the room
number."

"What's the address of the house?"

He told me, and answered a lot more questions along the same line, but
it wasn't getting me anywhere. He swore that so far as he knew there was
no particular connection between Aims and Eleanor La Tour, that no one
had known he was going to call for a girl that night. He knew Bronson from
past trips to town, and considered the salesman to be just what he appeared,
a traveling man with an eye for a blonde, not too particular how he met her.
As far as I could observe, the sweating house detective was telling the truth.
He didn't let anything slip, anyhow.

"How well do you know that red-headed waitress, Vera?" I asked him.

He winked at me. "Not so well as you do, from all I hear."

The humor of that escaped me, and I let him know it. He sobered up in a
hurry. I decided the louse must have a good thing in this job, he was so anxious to keep it.

"I know her pretty well," he said. "She's okay when she's not drinking,
but screwy after a few shots."

"How does she act?"

"She might act any way, from loving to cold-shoulder. But after a point
she always gets hard-boiled and claims somebody insulted her. I hear she
pulled that on you the other night."

He was sorry he said that last, as soon as it was out.

"What else did you hear about that night?" I demanded.

He shrugged. "Just that you went to the Arbor, and a couple of guys jumped you. And that you handle yourself fast for such a soft-spoken guy."

I gave his idea of a compliment the attention it deserved, which was none.

"Who were the two strong-arms?"

"I dunno, Marks, I swear I don't. Never saw them before."

"What do you mean, you never saw them before? When did you see them at all?"

Cramer was sweating profusely. "I don't mean nothin'," he said, turning sullen.

"I mean, that was a mistake. I just heard Vera and Mabel talking and they never saw them before."

I knocked the ashes out of my pipe and stood up. "Cramer," I said pleasantly, "I tried to play ball with you, but I don't like your curves. I'm going down now to talk to Hawkins. If he seems to be getting a slice of the cake, I'll try the directors."

"Wait a minute, Marks." He was on his feet too. "What will that get you? What do you gain by tripping me up, just because I don't know nothing? I swear to God that's the truth. This is blackmail!" He sounded shocked at the word.

"Sure it is. But it will get me the satisfaction of turning in a guy who two-times me when I'm willing to play along with him. Watch your hands!" I snapped suddenly, seeing him make a move toward a hip pocket. I was taking no chances — in his present state of mind I wouldn't have put it past the big ox to try knocking me off.

He quickly thrust both hands out in front of him and jumped back a good two feet. This time actual physical fear showed on his sweating red face.

"Marks, no! I'm not even packing a gun. See?" He turned his back and reached into the right hip pocket with exaggerated slowness, holding up the tail of his coat so that I could see the pocket was innocent of weapons. With thumb and forefinger he gingerly drew out a none too clean handkerchief. Then he collapsed in a chair and sat mopping his forehead.

I was surprised, not having figured him quite like that. Still, there I had it on a silver platter, so why pass it up? I flipped out the Mauser and pointed it in his general direction. "Where did you hear I could handle a gun?"

"Eddie Titano," he mumbled absently, watching the gun. Then he sat bolt upright as he realized what he had said.

I sat down again. "Cramer," I said evenly, "just one more chance to talk straight. And from where I sit you may not just be talking yourself out of losing your job, but out of a murder rap."

He was sallow through the sweat. "Okay, Marks, here it is. I dropped into the Arbor Club this morning, and Aims told me about it. Titano was there having a drink. That's all I know. I just happened to be there."

"Tell me what Titano said, word for word."

"He was sore. He said he told Aims to be careful, that you were smooth with a gun."

Once again, Cramer realized too late what he had said.

"Like that, eh? Titano hired the deal for Hart?"

"I dunno. That's all I heard."

He was over his fright some by then, not quite so sluggish on the thought processes, so I tried another track. I put the gun away and said casually: "What time did Aims phone you?"

"About ten," he said. Then: "Damn you, Marks!"

"So he sent for you. What about?"

"He just wanted to know the low-down on Smallwood. I told them it was suicide."

"Suicide?" I asked. "With Aims hired to get the Colonel, and a girl from one of his houses on this floor when it was done?"

"Look, Marks," he said earnestly, "this time I'm leveling with you. You may be right about that, but I doubt it. They seemed awfully surprised. The way they told it, Hart just wanted to beat up the old boy for a warning. He got in touch with Aims for those two punks. If the killing wasn't news to them, they put on a damn good act, and they didn't need an act with me. They didn't even need to bring me into it."

Which last was true, of course. I kept at him for a time, but the pay dirt had been panned out. He stuck to that story without lapse or deviation. I switched again.

"What about Mabel? Was she in on the deal?"

"I don't think so. She's pretty much on the up and up. Likes to pick up a dollar now and then, naturally. I think Aims just saw her with you guys and told her to bring you over to his place for a percentage of the take."

"What about the elevator girls? Would they be telling the truth about not bringing anybody up?"

"How would I know? But I don't see why not. The older one has been here a hundred years, and kept her nose clean. Esther Taylor's just a kid only been here a couple of months, and high-hat as the devil. Won't even pass the time of day with the rest of the help. I can't see her palling around with any hoodlums, or telling a false story for them."

That was the way she had struck me. Sort of the social register set among elevator girls. She appeared extremely unlikely to be a member of Aims' or Hart's set-up.

"Okay, Cramer," I said finally. "I guess that's all now. Keep me posted if anything turns up."

"Sure, sure," he told me, lying in his teeth. He looked pale and wilted but no longer so worried.

"Just one more thing — what about this kid Jerry, the bellhop? What's he like?"

Cramer paused with his hand on the door. He spoke definitely, and with more assurance than I had yet heard him use. "Now there, Marks, is one smart kid. He'll go a long way in the world. If you get a chance to use him, do it."

He gave me a broad wink and shut the door behind him. That made one point on which Cramer and I agreed one hundred percent.

CHAPTER TEN

THE TALK with the house detective had taken a long time, so that it was six o'clock when I got out of a cab at the door of the Arbor Club. It was dimly lit, with the neon sign not turned on. Obviously the place was not yet open for its evening business. That, definitely, was not good. I would have preferred to talk to Aims in the light of considerable publicity.

Still, there I was and I didn't intend just to drive on back. I took a swift look at the gum-chewing, bored-appearing cab driver and decided to take a chance on him. I had been careful to hail a roving cab rather than climb into the line at the hotel.

"That'll be a buck," he said.

I pulled out a five-dollar bill and handed it to him. "Here's half your fare," I told him. "You get the other half when I come out. And don't let anyone tell you I won't be out — you just sit right here and wait for me."

A glint of interest came into his eyes as he took the bill. He reached to the floor at his feet and came up with a hefty wrench which he put on the seat beside him. "Don't worry," he said. "I'll be here five dollars' worth, anyhow."

The Club's front door was closed but not locked. I stepped inside without being challenged. There was no one in the entrance hall. A couple of waiters were shuffling around the tables inside, not paying any attention to the red-headed girl and the piano player who were rehearsing their act for the floor show. I watched for a moment while getting my bearings.

The musician was playing "A Pretty Girl Is Like A Melody," very slowly, and as far as I could tell, quite badly. He was only using one hand, and seemed on the point of going to sleep at the piano. The girl was revolving deliberately in what must have been a dance, although I couldn't place the variety. She held one hand in front of her, one behind. Her black slacks were too tight for her impressive hips; her green sweater only partially concealed a mountainous bosom. She wasn't exactly fat but she was a really big girl. I got the routine as the music ended and she stood still, holding both hands high above her head. She was a fan dancer, rehearsing without benefit of props. I decided to catch that floor show sometime. It must be quite an act.

I walked to the door that was half-hidden by the fake trees, still not noticed by anyone in the place. I pushed it open and stepped quickly inside.

Aims, looking up sharply from his seat behind the desk, didn't betray surprise by the flicker of an eyelash. This man was no Cramer.

"Just dropped in for a talk," I said, taking a chair at the side of the desk, where I could watch both him and the door.

"All right, Marks, what do we talk about?" He seemed entirely at ease, and his voice had lost the veiled hostility of our last meeting.

"Murder will be a good subject. That's the kind of case I'm working on now, anyhow."

He showed his teeth at me, probably meaning it for a smile. "Murder, Marks? That's interesting. Especially since the cops don't seem to be taking it that way. You wouldn't mean suicide, would you?"

"Look, Aims," I said, "we can make this tough or easy. I don't give a damn what the police call it. Colonel Smallwood was a Watson client. He got knocked off. That makes it our business to the finish. Wait a minute" — as he started to speak — "you've got something I want, and it may be to your advantage to play ball with me. If you had him killed, I don't expect you to talk. If you didn't, you'll be better off to help me clear it up. I'm talking about the murder only, understand. I'm not interested in assault or red light houses or anything else, though those things might come in for quite a bit of publicity if we have to dig too deep into your affairs."

There was a hard glint in his eye. "Big talk for one private dick, Marks."

"One private dick, nothing. Watson will throw twenty men in here in twenty-four hours if it comes to that. Ask Lucky Hart if it's a good idea to fool around with us just for fun."

He stared at me a minute without speaking, and I had a pretty good idea that he had already discussed with Hart the question of how much he needed to take from me.

"What about it, Aims? Did you kill him yourself, or are you willing to play ball?"

He grinned suddenly. "Sort of a 'have you stopped beating your wife' question, isn't it? But I've nothing to lose by playing along with you. None of my boys killed him, and I don't know who did. Or if anyone did. It sounds like suicide, from what I've heard. I'll be frank with you. Hart says your agency pulls a lot of water in your home town, and so you have a certain nuisance value. Ask me what you want to know."

"I want to know why those two thugs jumped us in here on Saturday night." When his eyes veiled on me again, I added: "Just the two of us are here, remember. No mikes or witnesses. I just want the straight of it."

Aims shrugged his shoulders. "As you say, no witnesses. I'll deny saying it, of course. Lucky Hart told me the old gent lifted a pile from him in a game. He wanted it back, and wanted to prove he meant business. He didn't want to use either of the boys out here with him, so he asked me to pick up a couple. I did — the two you saw. Their orders were to rough him up, but nothing serious. Joe was supposed to take care of you. Joe," with a faint smile, "is a little sore at you, Marks. He hasn't my forgiving nature." He rubbed his hand reflectively over the lump on his head.

"Who were the two guys, and where are they now?"

"Just a couple of punks. They got out of town when they heard about the killing. I wouldn't know where they are now."

"So that's it, is it?" I said nastily. "You're going to be a good guy. You tell me what I already know, and let me whistle for the rest. Do you really think I can't find them? I just thought we were doing it the easy way."

He was a smooth article, not letting his face give away a thing, but I knew his mind was sorting over all the ways there were to trace them. The help in the Arbor Club, the unreliable Cramer, the dozen other leads he hadn't troubled to cover on what to him had been a minor affair. I stared right back at him, and after a pause he gave me a couple of names, and an address in Denver. Then he let his generally expressionless face show his animosity while his voice turned ugly.

"This is just for your crowd, Marks. Look up those boys if you want to, but if you put the cops into them, I swear I'll rub you out. With no leads left, either. Your nuisance value can come at too high a price, and don't forget it."

I wasn't forgetting it, not for a minute. It was impossible to know what was in Aims' secretive mind, just what skeletons he might fear my unearthing. Or how deeply he was really involved in the Colonel's death, for that matter. If at any time he decided I was more dangerous to him alive than dead, he would take the gamble. Dark alleys would hold no attraction for me until this affair was finished.

We talked for a time longer, entirely without result to me. The night club owner said nothing carelessly, nothing which he didn't consider and weigh beforehand.

He walked to the door of his office with me. I stepped aside to let him go through first, then followed. I found myself standing about six feet from Joe, the bouncer. He glared at me, his face contorted.

"Dammit, boss," he said, "is this guy on the payroll?"

Aims stepped to one side, a smile which looked genuine splitting his dead-pan. "He's nothing to me, one way or the other. Any argument you boys have is a private affair."

It took Joe a minute to get it. Then he jumped for me. I could have shot him, yes. There was time for that if I really wanted to nail him, but the last thing I wanted there was a killing, as Aims knew very well. And Joe didn't want to kill me, probably. He just meant to beat the stuffing out of me for that crack on the head, and the ribbing he must have taken because of it.

I met him halfway, chopping down hard with the side of my hand at his neck, but his shoulder caught most of the force of the blow. He twisted sideways and stopped with his hip the knee I threw at his stomach, and then a couple of bombs cracked me along the waistline as he let go with both hands. I heard Aims' voice say, "Outside, no rough stuff around the furniture," as I grabbed Joe and held on to keep from falling. I had picked up a little judo in the army, but somewhere or other Joe had learned quite a bit more. He slammed me against the door hard enough to rattle the wall.

"How do you like it, sport?" he yelled, and came for me again. That comment gave me the split-second's time I needed. I met him and let him grab; then I brought the blackjack up and over. This time there was considerable enthusiasm behind it, with no thought of carefully calculated damage. He went down like a rock.

The outer door opened with a jerk. There stood my cab driver, wrench in hand. "You need me, chief?" he asked.

I leaned against the wall, breathing hard and conscious that I would be sore for a week. I was considerably madder at Aims for not stopping it than I was at the man on the floor. Joe, after all, might well be said to have his reasons for what he did.

"Maybe I do," I said. "How about it, Aims? Do I need him?" The two waiters were on the scene behind Aims, neither with empty hands. A door slammed somewhere out back.

Aims looked entirely unconcerned. "No," he said, "I think Joe is out for the day. Too bad, but no need for this to disturb our agreement. You might as well go on home."

He was right, and we went.

CHAPTER ELEVEN

I WENT BACK to the hotel, feeling the need for dinner and a bath before carrying the matter any further. Things didn't seem to be breaking my way. I was picking up information here and there, but I was absorbing a lot more physically than I was mentally. There seemed to be some indication that I might break before the case did.

A glance at my reflection in the plate glass window of the hotel lobby surprised me. I looked just about as always, with no indication of the recent bouncing around. Well, I didn't feel as always. I was sore in body and spirit, and lacked the satisfaction of having made any particular progress. I punched the elevator button with unnecessary vigor.

Inside the elevator came another surprise. The night operator, the brunette kid Cramer called Esther Taylor, was alone. She gave me a long, slow look, making like Lauren Bacall, and smiled at me. "Hello, Mr. Marks," she said companionably. More than companionably, in fact. Both the tone and the look held a challenge and a promise.

This was interesting. I gave her shoulder a tentative pat, and the result of that was interesting, too. Instead of giving me the quick freeze with which she had greeted a similar gesture from the Colonel, she sort of snuggled her shoulder up against my hand. That may not sound possible, but believe me, it is. A pleasant sensation, too.

We rode like that for several floors. Stopping at the eighth, she kept the door shut for a few seconds while she gave me another one of those long, sultry looks. "I think being a detective must be simply thrilling, Mr. Marks." The words came out in a breathless sort of rush.

"You do, huh?" She just flickered her eyelashes at me, ignoring a buzz from the third floor.

"Are you making any progress on your case?" she asked.

The buzzer sounded again, someone really leaning on it this time. She sighed and opened the door. "We'll get together and talk it over some-time," I suggested as I stepped out. Her "I'd love to," came back to me just as she started the car down.

I thought that matter over while I took a bath and shaved. First Miss Jensen, then this younger and more shapely edition, putting on the same act. I might be taking a mauling from the men connected with this case, but I was sure impressing the fair sex.

Lucky Hart was staying at the Astoria Hotel. I had picked that up from Sergeant Thomas. A visit with him seemed in order, although I was probably sticking my neck out again. I decided to have a quick snack and catch him at the hotel before he went out for the evening.

In the hall, Corporal Stevens was pushing the elevator button. He looked rumpled, as though he had only recently gotten up from the chair we had left him in last night. Well, he had been carrying enough of a load to sleep the clock around. Now he seemed fairly fresh, though with dark circles still under his eyes. He gave me a friendly grin which held no hint of recognition.

The grin broadened when we got into the elevator. "Hello, honey," he said to the girl. "Nice evening."

She gave him an icy stare. "Isn't it?" she said. When her glance met mine, she drooped one eyelid at me.

As I came out onto the street from the hotel, I took a quick look around, more from habit than with any thought of danger. I was glad I did. When I had climbed back into my cab in front of the Arbor Club, a nondescript sort of little man in a dark suit had been leaning against a tree, picking his teeth. He hadn't seemed to take any particular interest in me and hadn't really registered on my mind. But here he was again, sitting in a car as neutral and unremarkable as himself, parked about twenty feet down the street. He was reading a newspaper.

I walked down the street, keeping a careful eye on him as I sauntered along. He pulled out from the curb after I had gone about half a block, trailing me. I stepped into a hamburger joint and took a booth at the back. For the next twenty minutes my thoughts were divided between him and my steak, with the steak getting the most attention. There is no point in letting your work spoil your appetite.

When I went up front to pay the check, he was sitting at the counter, drinking a cup of coffee. I sized him up carefully. He didn't look like much of anything, but he was packing a gun in his hip pocket. Through the glass of the entrance door, I could see his gray coupé standing at the curb. I picked up my change and then clapped him on the shoulder.

"Okay, pal," I said, "let's go. The coffee is on me." I tossed a dime to the cashier and went out and climbed in the car.

He followed me. "Look, bud," he said, talking tough, "I don't know you. You got me mixed up with somebody."

"We have mutual friends. Get in and we'll talk about Sergeant Thomas."

He grinned and walked around to the driver's side. "Okay, wise guy. How did you spot me?"

I pointed to the water hydrant beside the car. "Who but a cop would park beside a fire-plug on a main street?"

He scowled at me. "Thomas said you were quite a joker. Okay, ha ha. Now get going about your business so I can tail you."

"I'm just going down to the Astoria. Be a good guy and drive me there. The taxpayers won't mind an extra passenger. You know," I added as he started to refuse, "Thomas would get a kick out of your pulling a rookie stunt like parking by that plug, wouldn't he? Maybe we better not tell him I spotted you."

He looked at me speculatively. "Maybe not. And don't tell him I'm running a taxi service for you, either. Astoria, you say?"

He wasn't a bad guy. His name was Edgar Holt and he had three kids and he had been doing plainclothes stuff two years. I wondered how he ever got any information when he never stopped talking himself.

"Drop me here," I said, when we were a block from Hart's hotel. "Some people might get the wrong idea seeing me running around with cops. Wait for me and we'll have a couple of beers."

"Okay. I'll be in the loading zone across the street. Don't cross me up, now!"

I promised and got out, walking the rest of the way to the hotel alone. The Astoria was the town's largest, with a lobby that would double nicely for Grand Central Station. As I approached the desk, a bell hop eyed me carefully and let me pass, deciding by some secret process of his own that there was no profit for him there. The clerk asked "Yes?" in a determinedly polite tone which said plainly enough that he had a lot of more important things he should be doing.

I asked him to ring Mr. Hart's room and say that Mr. Marks wanted to see him. I spelled the name — M A R K S — because that was an item it might possibly be important for him to remember. He strolled over to the switchboard and appeared to forget all about me. Eventually he came back and told me that Mr. Hart would see me if I went right up to Room 1125. He beckoned a bell boy to show the way.

In the elevator that youth grinned companionably and asked if I were a stranger in town.

I told him that I was. He winked and said that he could suggest some good spots to finish out the evening. If my luck held out, he said, just ask for Pete when I left and he would fix me up. Lucky Hart didn't appear to be keeping his game under wraps at this stand.

At the door of 1125 Pete rapped out some sort of code of his own. It was opened immediately by the big muscle man who had been with Hart at our hotel. He gave me a toothy smile.

"Well, well, if it ain't the big shot himself. Hold it," he added, seeing me reach for a coin, "I take care of all that here." He flipped a half-dollar into

Pete's outstretched hand. That made the kid exactly forty cents better off than he would have been with me taking care of him.

I walked into the room shepherded by the door keeper, who didn't let me get six inches away from him. The front room of the suite was set up for a card game, with a round table, poker chips, and seven straight chairs taking up one side. Lucky Hart sat in an easy chair, smoking a cigar. The little gunman, Titano, stood by the window.

Hart gave me a salute with the cigar. "Have a chair, Marks. What's on your mind?"

His voice wasn't friendly and it wasn't unfriendly. Noncommittal would be the right word for it. Titano was putting as much dislike into his unblinking stare as a look could hold. I took a chair.

"Just thought we might have a talk, Hart. We seem to have some interests in common."

"I'll talk to anyone, but I can't figure us having much in common. Cigar?"

I accepted the cigar. The big boy held a match for me, and placed an ash try at my elbow. He reminded me of a motherly spider getting a newly arrived fly comfortably settled. It was a very good cigar.

"Well," I said, "there was the Colonel. We both knew him."

"Yeah, so we did. But I hear he knocked himself off, so that leaves us right back where we started, doesn't it?"

"Did he knock himself off? I'm not so sure, and I don't think the cops are so sure, whatever they tell the papers."

Hart shrugged. "Either way, it makes no difference to me. I had a game going here all night, with some pretty solid citizens with me to prove it. I had an interest in him alive — a twenty-grand interest, in fact — but I guess that's water over the dam now. You were no help to me on that little deal, now were you, Marks?"

The hop-head by the window made a snarling noise deep in his throat. I said to Hart: "Do you pay Eddie on commission? He seems to be taking a personal sort of interest in missing that collection."

Hart's smile didn't move any muscles but those at the corner of his mouth. "His professional pride is hurt. He has the idea that only a .45 slug in your guts will make him feel better. I tell him that's foolish — that you just made a mistake, and that now you are through sticking your nose into our business. Am I right?"

"Before he gets too upset, you'd better tell him that the desk clerk sent me up by name, and that I have an appointment with the homicide squad in the morning. I think one of their boys trailed me here, too."

I wasn't entirely enjoying that cigar. It was to Hart's interest to avoid trouble there in his room, and I wasn't worried about any move from him, but Titano was another matter. Any hop-head is unpredictable. I kept a careful eye on him.

"That's nothing to me. Like I told you, I'm alibied from here to breakfast. So speak your piece before my company comes."

"Okay, if you're clean, that's that. But tell me, Hart, do you keep these two characters in here with the suckers? Doesn't that give the place a rough atmosphere for a friendly game?"

"Eddie stays in the bedroom. He's just our insurance in case of trouble."

"So," I said, "you're alibied, but your trigger man might have been almost anywhere about the time the Colonel was killed — in the bedroom or out on the fire escape or what have you. You call that an alibi?"

The silence following that crack hurt my ears. The cigar was in my left hand; my left shoulder was sagging enough to let the coat lapel hang free of my body. I kept my attention centered on Titano, standing rigid by the window, his sallow face turning slowly ashen as the implication of the remark sank in. I figured the percentages were against trouble then, but if it was to come tonight, this would be it. If the hop-head went out of control, my life expectancy would be governed by whether or not I could flip the Mauser out and fire before he could dig for those big .45s.

Lucky Hart, sitting just out of arm's reach, didn't worry me too much. If his reputation could be believed, he didn't handle his own rough stuff. The idea of the big boy behind me wasn't pleasant. In a way it was a relief to hear his feet shuffle over the carpet as he moved to one side. And in another way it wasn't a relief — it showed that he read the killer look in Titano's eyes the same as I did, and was moving out of range.

It probably wasn't more than five seconds that Eddie and I sat there with our eyes boring into each other. It seemed an hour. I didn't know too much about Titano, except that he was supposed to be Hart's trigger man, and was said to like working at his job. Whether he was fast or slow, I had no idea, and I didn't relish finding out this way. I've never claimed to be a hero. I take no more chances than my business requires. I figured this was necessary, to jar them loose and get them to talking, but it was no pleasure. I felt cold sweat crawling under my collar.

Then Hart was on his feet between us, moving straight to Titano. The big fellow joined them with a rush. I released the breath I hadn't realized I was holding. Between them they got the gunman, twitching and hysterical, into the bedroom and closed the door behind them. A cigar had never tasted so good before as that next puff did.

Lucky Hart came back alone. "Marks," he said, "you are a fool." He sat down again, no longer relaxed and easy. His voice had changed little, his expression not at all, but he nevertheless showed anger where only cool indifference had been before.

I shrugged. "Anybody's a fool to be in this business, maybe. I don't like to have clients knocked off under my nose."

"So you figure it will help your pride to have Titano rub you out? And in my room, for God's sake!"

"Would he have rubbed me out, Hart? Or would I have gotten him, and then hung you for hiring him to kill the Colonel?"

Hart's voice was coldly furious. "If you really figure it that way, you're a bigger fool than I thought. I didn't have a hand in whatever happened to the old slicker; I interfered then just to stop trouble here in my room. Don't come here again."

"I might come back with a homicide man. How do you think he would figure your gunnie's nervousness on the subject?"

Hart had complete control of himself again, if he could be said to have ever lost it. "That might cause me some inconvenience," he admitted. "Maybe enough to get you found stiff in some alley when all this blows over. But what does it get you, Marks? Put your cards on the table — what do you want here?"

I told him what I wanted, leaving Aims' name out of it but letting him see that his part in the transaction was known to me. Hart listened quietly, drawing on his cigar with every appearance of casual unconcern. When he spoke, it was without heat.

"I might have had a hand in that affair at the Club Arbor," he admitted. "Maybe the boys misunderstood me and got too rough. I just told them to see about collecting the money I figured was coming to me. About the business at the hotel the next day, I don't know a thing. Why, killing him was the last thing I wanted. He's no good to me dead. Mine isn't the kind of bill I can put in a claim for against his estate."

I couldn't budge him from that. It might have been the truth and it might not, but unquestionably it had the virtue of common sense. I couldn't picture him having the Colonel knocked off without more of an attempt to collect from him. There was, of course, the possibility that he had been killed in a final collection attempt that went wrong.

"Okay, Hart," I said, "just one thing more. You made a crack to him about San Francisco the first night we saw you here. Tell me the story on that."

"It isn't much of a story." He shrugged. "You may as well believe me, Marks, when I say I didn't know the old man at all. He really fooled me in that one game. I played him for what he pretended to be, a rich old sucker out for a night's fun. He took me to the cleaners. After that I made inquiries, naturally. He was strictly a small-time operator. Played vacation resorts, hotels, sometimes the boats. He never tangled with the smart money before that I know of. One of my boys used to know him in Frisco, twenty years or so ago. Said he ran a club there, with a partner. One night there was some trouble and the Colonel plugged a guy. My man couldn't remember much about it, but he said it made some stink in Frisco at the time."

"Did the fellow die?"

"Tony didn't remember. He didn't even remember either of their names, except that he was pretty sure the old boy was going by a different one then. He never knew him well — just saw him around some."

"Do you know anybody besides yourself who might have had it in for the old man?"

"On the level, I don't. In his business he must have had a hundred guys with a reason to see him rubbed out, but from what I heard he didn't generally take on the class of people who would do that."

"Except for you," I said.

Hart lit another cigar. "I think we're through, Marks," he said. "I've told you what I know, and I've told it straight. If you are really trying to clear it up, I wish you luck. If you're trying to pin it on me, you won't be able to. And don't try any fast ones. I'd rather get along with you than not, because it's easier, but if you really get in my hair I'll see to it that you're taken out — permanently."

So that made two promises of that sort for the day, both by parties who meant it, had the organization to try it, and wouldn't lose any sleep over the accomplishment. I had the feeling that there must be a more pleasant way to make a living than the racket I was in. I said goodbye and left, knowing very little more than in the beginning.

I punched the elevator bell. While I was standing there waiting for the car to come, a nondescript little figure strolled around the corner of the corridor to join me. It was Edgar, the plainclothesman, wearing his usual vacant expression.

"Have a nice visit?" he asked.

"Edgar," I said, "have I made a mistake in you?"

"No mistake at all. You figured I was put on your tail and that's right where I am. The sarge wouldn't have liked having you in there with that kind of company and me not around."

"What good would you have done me out in the hall?" I asked.

"That isn't exactly the idea," Edgar explained. "The sarge wouldn't so much have minded you having an accident. He just wouldn't have liked it if I couldn't have nailed the guy who did it. How about that beer?"

CHAPTER TWELVE

I RANG THE BELL captain and asked him to send Jerry up. When I opened
the door to the kid, his appearance wasn't up to its usual standard. The old
worldly wise expression tried for a place on his features, but didn't quite
make it. He shifted from one foot to the other while he waited for me to say
something, and it dawned on me that Jerry, through some devious reasoning
of his own, didn't believe the Colonel was a suicide. He thought it was
murder, and he figured that I had done the killing. As a result he was scared
to death to be alone in the same room with me.

"Have a chair," I suggested.

"No, thanks," he said, his voice a wavering line. "I mean, I gotta get
back to work. If it's okay with you, that is."

A polite Jerry was an odd spectacle. It wasn't becoming to him, somehow.
Too much out of character. "Okay, stand up then. I want you to do something for me."

"Sure, sure, anything at all."

"I want to talk to the waitress, Mabel, without a lot of people knowing
about it."

From the quick suspicion that jumped into his eyes, it was plain that he
was picturing Mabel being carved up in the bathtub. I finally got him to
agree to go down and ask her to stop by the room for a few minutes, but it
took tact, bribery, and a considerable amount of intimidation to get his
promise.

Just as he left the phone rang, a collect call from San Francisco. I agreed
to accept the charges and soon heard the deep tones Charley Sloan uses
when he is trying to disguise his voice.

"Mr. Marks," the sonorous voice said, "this is Alfred P. Higgenbottom
of San Francisco."

"Why the devil didn't you put this on your own swindle sheet?" I asked
irritably. "And don't be so junior G-man. Anybody listening to this call is
welcome to it."

"Okay, okay," Charley said in his natural voice. "Keep your shirt on. I
figured it might be hush-hush."

"It's on the way to being hushed up from hell to breakfast. Did you get
anything?"

"Some. That character you were with was no Sunday School teacher. He was tangled up in a shooting here back in the twenties, like you figured. You need me up there?"

"Can't think of anything I need less. You sure you got all the dope on the Colonel? I might give you a tip or so."

"I got it," Charley said, and I believed him. "Don't tell me anything that's going to strain your generosity. Shall I mail it up?"

"Yeah, air mail. I'm trying to get in touch with a guy named Hector P. Curtis for the boss. On the Williams matter. You tell the old man I'm expecting Curtis to call me sometime tomorrow."

Hector P. Curtis was another of Charley's aliases. He claimed that a name like Smith sounded too suspicious. I was sure he would get the idea, which was that I wanted him on the job here, promptly and privately. Charley as a mental giant might be open to criticism from some sources, but Charley and his short-barrelled .32 struck me as exactly what I needed to keep the hot breath of Aims and Hart and company off the back of my neck.

"Okay," Charley said. "Be seeing you. Try not to get any powder burns from clients being shot too close to you."

He hung up then, which was smart of him, and left me swearing purely for the benefit of whomever Sergeant Thomas might have listening in.

Mabel came shortly, signalling her arrival with a timid rap on the door. When I opened it she gave me a tentative smile, not scared, but uncertain just what this was all about. I seated her in the big chair where we had found the Colonel and offered her a drink. She refused on the ground of having to go back to work.

"Gee," she said, "these rooms are swell, aren't they? I mean, it seems so sort of refined to be in a hotel room that doesn't have a bed."

I agreed that a bed was most unrefined. She said that she was awfully sorry about the old gentleman shooting himself. She said he had been a real sport. She asked if it had been an accident. Eventually she worked herself up to the question which had been uppermost in her mind all along. She wanted to see the place where the body had been found.

"He was sitting right where you are, right in that chair."

I didn't get the shriek which, heel that I am, I was expecting. Her face went pale under its pancake makeup, and she got out of the chair, slowly and with some dignity, and stood in the middle of the room. "Mr. Marks," she said severely, "that wasn't a bit nice of you."

That was too true to admit any argument. I finally got her seated again, on the couch this time, so we could talk. She appeared more insulted than scared.

"Mabel," I said, "how did you happen to go out with us the other night?"

"You know, the old gentleman asked me, and I like a good time as well as the next girl. I thought you seemed like real nice refined fellows. Vera thought so too."

"Had you ever seen the Colonel before?"

"No, of course not."

"Had anybody ever talked to you about him?"

"Not until afterwards. Some cop talked to me then. What is all this, anyhow?"

"How did you happen to suggest going to the Club Arbor?"

"I just thought it was a good place to go for a good time."

I whipped out the leather folder I carry my credentials in, complete with picture, and passed it quickly in front of her eyes. From the look she got at it I might have been anything from an FBI man to a member of the musicians' union.

"That won't do, Mabel," I told her. "I saw you talking to Aims."

She started to cry a little bit. I couldn't tell whether it was from fright or just because she was a ready crier. The latter seemed more likely.

"That's true," she said through her sniffles. "Mr. Aims did tell me that if I brought my party out to his place he would see that I got a commission. There wasn't any harm in that, was there? It didn't cost you fellows any more."

"It nearly cost the Colonel a knock in the head. Doesn't that seem like harm to you?"

She stared at me. "Oh, no, that wasn't because we went there, was it? That was just because of Vera."

"You mean you didn't know there was going to be trouble at the Arbor Club?"

"Honest, Mr. Marks, I thought Roscoe Aims just wanted us to come there because it would bring him business. I've done that before, and everything was lovely. Only . . ." Her voice, which had carried conviction, died away.

"Only what?"

"I just remembered that the last time he told Vera never to come back again, because she always made a fuss. The other night he saw she was with us but he never said a word about her not coming."

"You mean Vera always acted like that?"

A look that might have been embarrassment showed on Mabel's chubby, unintelligent face. "She can't carry her liquor, and that's the truth. She usually raises an awful fuss when a fellow makes a pass at her. I tell her to be sensible and handle it quietly, like I do. After all, she might as well expect it — rich guys like you and the old gentleman don't take girls like us out unless they are on the make, and she knows it as well as I do."

A man in my business needs to develop a thick skin, so I let that go. "Then anyone who knew Vera could be pretty sure there would be a commotion of some kind when she got drunk enough?"

I made up my mind that she was telling the truth, and that she and Vera had been used as the innocent, to put a rather loose interpretation on the word, means of putting the finger on the Colonel.

I thanked her and let her go on back to work. It would have been good business to double-check my impressions by a talk with Vera before they had a chance to compare notes, but I let it go. The agency wasn't paying me that kind of money. It took very little imagination to picture the story Vera could build around a private session in my hotel room. Then I remembered those experimental pats I had given the elevator girl, purely for research purposes. I hoped that she wasn't inclined to chat too much.

There was a rap on the door. I felt the back of my neck prickle with an urgent, though indefinable, sense of trouble. The thought flashed that the Colonel might have heard a knock like that, crossed the room, and opened the door to his murderer. I had the Mauser in my hand as I got up.

"Who is it?" I asked through the door.

"Bellhop," was the answer. "Telegram left down at the desk for Mr. Marks."

The voice was ordinary enough, but something was wrong. The phrase "bellhop" didn't quite ring true. Other people called him that, but it didn't seem to me that I had ever heard one announce himself as other than "bell-boy." In a chancy business like mine you sometimes follow your hunches. I turned the key in the door and stepped back behind the open door of the clothes closet, where I could have a quick look at whoever came in from the hallway before his eyes found me. My thumb loosed the safety catch as I said, "Come in."

It was a legitimate bellboy who entered, telegram in hand, a red-headed kid whom I had seen around the hotel before. He was grinning, and his eyes were sharp with curiosity, until he located me standing there holding the gun on him. Then the grin dissolved into quite understandable terror.

"Thanks," I said, as casually as I could make it, taking the telegram from the tray in his shaking hand. I dropped the gun negligently into a pocket. "Excuse me. I was just cleaning this, and forgot I was holding it."

I gave him a dollar as a salve to my conscience. He took it and got out, and it seemed unlikely that anyone would ever talk him into delivering a telegram to me again.

The telegram was from William Watson, reminding me that the office liked to have a telegraphed report now and then.

CHAPTER THIRTEEN

I FELT GOOD the next morning, which bore out my theory that eight hours sleep will do more for you than a clear conscience. On the record of my accomplishments I should have felt lousy. The hopeful attitude carried through shaving, dressing and going downstairs for breakfast.

In the hotel coffee shop I amused myself trying to pick out Edgar's relief while I waited for ham and eggs. Edgar had told me he himself came on at noon. If it was anyone in that coffee shop, he had me fooled. The waitress who served me, a cute kid with a sprinkling of freckles across her nose, carefully stayed on the other side of the table when she brought my food. I figured Vera had spread my reputation to the morning shift.

When I had finished, I wandered out into the lobby, still trying to identify Edgar Jr. I didn't really care too much who he was, but it seemed a good excuse to sit still for an after breakfast cigar. Walking around ruins it for me.

After ten minutes or so I threw the cigar away and went outside. I hadn't picked out the tail, and the smoke was ruined anyhow, since you can't indulge in the Colonel's brand for two weeks and switch back to mine without feeling the shock. I stood on the curb watching the traffic and trying to decide what to do.

Nothing in the shape of brilliant detection presented itself, but some kind of action seemed indicated while waiting for Charley Sloan's report, especially since Charley's news probably wouldn't have much of anything to do with the case anyway. I decided to go to see Thomas.

On the bus going down to headquarters I entered a buck for taxi fare in my expense book. We all did it. I think Watson did it himself, on the theory that it helped out some way or other with his income tax.

The only people who got on the bus with me were a middle-aged fat woman, a blonde girl carrying a baby, and a hard-faced man of about thirty who filled the bill right down to his flat feet. He sat down half a dozen seats behind me, which I considered a smart play until he got off six blocks later and it was obvious that he had just wanted to be near the rear door.

Thomas happened to be in, which was nothing but pure luck. I never have been able to figure out the hours cops work. He looked a little pained to see me, but didn't throw me out. Miss Jensen beamed.

"How you doing?" Thomas asked. I gave that the answer it deserved by silently lighting a pipe after getting settled in the chair he hadn't asked me to take.

"Any luck on that string proposition with the doors?" he wanted to know. I couldn't ruin Miss Jensen's faith by telling him to go chase himself. She shuffled papers around in a filing cabinet, waiting for me to be brilliant. I said no luck.

"Have you tried the perspiration test on that glove?" I asked him. I was proud of that for an off-the-cuff shot.

"Perspiration test?"

"Sure, to see if anyone else wore it before the Colonel did. You guys have a complete lab here, don't you?"

Miss Jensen gave him a disgusted look.

"Oh, that." Thomas seemed enlightened. "We don't call it that here. No, we tried, but I was sure it wouldn't work on that kind of leather. Picks up too much moisture being handled in the store."

I think myself it would have sounded better without that last sentence, but Miss Jensen lapped it up, looking actually proud of him. And I never have been one hundred percent sure there wasn't some such test.

"Got anything else to suggest?" he asked. "We always like to get tips from you big-city operators."

"Yeah," I said. "I'd like to have Briggs' fingerprints. The Caldwell butler."

"I know who Briggs is," he told me. His tone didn't change, but he wasn't fooling around any more. "Why not Caldwell's own prints? That's all for now, Miss Jensen." He tossed that over his shoulder. She didn't go out quick, but she went, and shut the door behind her.

"I'd like Caldwell's prints too. And I wouldn't mind checking Hansen's. There is something behind this that might come out if we knew everything about everybody in it."

"Look, Marks, I've told you that's out." Thomas wasn't talking tough, and he didn't look too proud of himself, but he looked right at me. "I can't check Caldwell's prints without word getting back to him. I'm not ready to buck that until you can show me he has a hand in this. Or at least until you can prove the old guy didn't shoot himself."

"And the same for Briggs? A record stands out all over him."

"The same for Briggs. Sure, he probably has a record. Caldwell plays against some tough people, and Briggs is his bodyguard. Proving Briggs ran whiskey in '26 doesn't prove he was mixed up with killing your client in '50."

"What about his gun permit? You have his prints for that, don't you?"

Thomas took a minute to get his pipe going. "Does Briggs carry a gun?" he asked. "That's an angle for me to work on. I might get myself promoted proving Caldwell's bodyguard carries a gun without a permit."

"You go to hell," I said, without much irritation. "I'll go do some detecting."

"You can look him up in our files," he offered.

"Sure," I agreed. "You suggest I look under B for Briggs?" I started for the door.

He spoke just before I opened the door. "Show me how Briggs might have used that gun, Marks, and we'll give it the full treatment." I believed him.

I asked the cop at the traffic desk where the public library was. That seemed to surprise him some, but he told me politely.

Once in the library, I went to the newspaper stacks with some sort of an idea of finding out about the Caldwell family. Starting from 1920, there are more issues of one newspaper than you would think. An hour or so didn't teach me much except that the football scores were a lot lower in those days. About twelve-thirty I gave it up and went outside.

Edgar was sitting there in his old car, parked by a fire hydrant again. I gave it a look as I walked up and got in.

"Where else would I park?" he demanded. "I'd be a lot more conspicuous double-parked."

Maybe he was right, at that. I've never tried to tail a man in a car.

On the way back to the hotel, Edgar gave me various comprehensive details about his family and professional life. "Aren't you supposed to shut up and listen sometimes?" I asked him. "Aren't you supposed to pump me? How are you going to find out what I know if you don't ever listen?"

Edgar spat out the open window. "Thomas does all the thinking, and he says you don't know anything. Besides, if you did let something slip, what would I do with it? I ain't even supposed to be talking to you."

That left my score for matching wits with the police department at about zero for the day. "Who is your relief, Edgar?" I asked.

"You mean you ain't spotted him, Detective?" That seemed to please Edgar.

"Okay, keep it to yourself. That will make him look better when I ask Thomas why he keeps an undersized little tail on me from noon on and lets me run around by myself mornings."

Edgar thought about that for a couple of blocks. "That's a sneaky stunt," he announced. "He's a colored boy, name of Willie Smith. Drives a '41 Cadillac coupé." That sure was one humorous police department.

In the lobby of the Essex was a sight that might not have made an impression on anyone else in town but that surely looked good to me. Charley Sloan was about forty years old, not tall, with a mournful face that pretty well reflected his disposition. He didn't pay much money for his clothes and he wore them a long while. He seldom had them pressed, either, which might have explained why the short-barrelled .32 he carried in the waistband of his pants didn't show. He sat there in the lobby reading his newspaper and looking as though the news didn't suit him too well.

I strolled past and went into the men's room at the end of the lobby, which proved to be empty. Charley wandered in a few minutes later.

"How are you, big shot?" he asked. "The boss said I'd probably run into you in a place like this." We shook hands. "Am I supposed to pretend I don't know you?"

"Yeah, I think we better keep it under cover. Where are you staying?"

He named a hotel. "What's so secret about it?"

"I don't know," I admitted, "but you never can tell." I knew all right — it was more comfortable to have Charley around as an unknown bodyguard than sitting there as a clay pigeon beside me. "I'll see you at the hotel after lunch."

As Charley left the room, Jerry the bell boy came in. "What you doing here?" he demanded. "Ain't the can in your room good enough for you? Or do you think maybe Vera won't chase you in here?" I told him that with his sense of humor he should be on the police force.

One way and another I had had enough of the employees of that hotel for the moment, so I went a block down the street to a hamburger stand. I had a hamburger, coffee and pie, entered a dollar and a quarter for lunch in my expense book, and was out of the joint in fifteen minutes. The waitress there gave me the complete lack of attention I had always received from women until Vera's comments singled me out.

Edgar was sitting in his car half a block down the street, looking annoyed. "Why didn't you say where you were going, and I wouldn't have bothered to move the bus. And I could have had lunch myself."

"You're on duty. How about driving me downtown to a big department store?"

Edgar wanted to know why it had to be a big one. He doubted that I wanted to buy anything I couldn't get close by. I doubted that the police department was going to tell me where to do my shopping. We bickered about it until we hit the business district, where Edgar pulled up at a loading zone in front of a store which occupied the entire block.

"Big enough for you?" he asked.

I thanked him and got out. Edgar got out too. This was another of my slow days, as I hadn't thought of that. "You wait here," I told him. "I want to buy something intimate."

"I better help you," he said. "This is a big town that a stranger might get lost in." We went into the store together.

I would have hated to have had any of the other boys from the office watching during the next half-hour. It is fairly easy to ditch a tail if he has to stay far enough behind you and sufficiently inconspicuous to keep from being spotted. Trying to ditch one who walks along beside you borrowing matches and talking politics is something else again. I tried the elevator dodge, thick crowds, sudden corners, everything I could think of. No sale. Short of breaking into a dead run, I couldn't shake Edgar, and even at that I wasn't so sure he might not have caught me.

"Edgar," I said finally, "this is no good for either of us. I can't do any detecting with you for a chaperone, and you can't find out anything from me until I pick something up."

He looked at me placidly. "Thomas says you ain't going to find out anything, except maybe that a town Lucky Hart is in ain't a lucky town for you. My orders are to be on hand if anybody happens to rub you out."

"I give up," I said. "Let's go back to the hotel."

Back at the car, Edgar took his keys out of his pocket and unlocked the door. As he opened it, I picked the keys out of his fingers with my left hand, placed my right on his chest and my foot behind him and pushed firmly. I flipped the catch on the door behind me as I got in, the motor started fast, and that was all there was to it. It wasn't so old a model that it had a running board to jump on; I had been pretty sure Edgar didn't have orders to go so far as to shoot; and not many men will shove their hand through a pane of glass on the spur of the moment. Edgar just stood there and waved at me as I went around the next corner, through a red light.

CHAPTER FOURTEEN

I LEFT THE CAR a couple of blocks up the street, parked beside a fire hydrant. That seemed to be one place he would think of looking, and I didn't want to cause him a lot of trouble. I was in Charley's hotel room ten minutes later. When Charley wanted to know what had kept me so long, I told him it had been a slow lunch.

I filled in the story from the time I joined the Colonel to date. Charley sat there picking his teeth and looking uninterested, which he probably was, but he heard what I was saying and he would remember it. If he saw one of the people I was describing, he would recognize him and have a pretty good idea what to do about it. So far as the deep thinking was concerned, that was supposed to be my part of the job.

Then he told me what he had picked up in San Francisco. There had been a lot of shootings there in the '20s, of course, but the one that seemed the most likely to fill our bill concerned a Captain James, who had run a speakeasy and gambling room in partnership with a man named Jack Barlow. Both James and Barlow had been around forty years old in 1927. James had a wife, Mamie, considerably younger than he was, and a two-year-old daughter named Helen. Barlow was the brains of the deal, James the card operator. The "Captain" angle was generally considered to be a phony. That tied in with the Colonel, all right.

There had been a fight in the gambling room one night in 1927, and the Captain had blasted a customer who had pulled a knife over the turn of a card. The newspaper accounts showed a disagreement among the witnesses as to where he had gotten the gun. One said he took it from his pants pocket. Another claimed that a red-haired "gun moll" (the witness' words) handed it to him. Still a third said it seemed to jump out of his sleeve.

The Captain had left town suddenly, and although the customer hadn't died and there never was much heat about it, nothing more had been heard from either the Captain or Barlow. Or the wife and daughter either, for that matter. Maybe they weren't missing; maybe they were just staying out of the newspapers and away from the police. After all, it had been a long time ago. So far as Charley or his police department pal who gave him most of this dope knew, they could all have kept living right in Frisco.

Well, there it was, for what it was worth. We kicked it around for a while without deciding anything. There had been no pictures, and descriptions

84

were meager. Captain James could be Colonel Alexander Smallwood. Or anyone else with a sleeve gun. All in all, I was inclined to think the Colonel was James, grown older and smoother and with a natural increase in rank through the years.

Barlow could be Thornton Caldwell, although that was stretching it farther. The dignified Mrs. Caldwell could be Mrs. James, though it was hard to picture her as a girl named Mamie, wife of a small-time gambler. Briggs the butler was a shade young for any of the principals, and Jerry the bellhop seemed entirely in the clear. We decided to forget it, and sent downstairs for cold beer.

After a few bottles things looked brighter. "First, maybe," Charley said, "we better figure out how it was done. You don't suppose there could be anything to that pin and string angle?"

"I don't know," I said irritably. "It doesn't seem likely, but I'm no mechanic. Try it yourself tomorrow."

"What about the elevator girl?"

"Not unless she knows you're a detective. She never gave me a tumble until I got famous."

Charley got up and moved the rest of the beer to the other side of the room. "I mean, could she have gotten in the room? Could she have shot him herself?"

"She could have gotten in the room without any trouble," I agreed, "and maybe she would have had to shoot him to get out. But it doesn't look to me like that kind of shooting."

"Then it must have been one of those characters on the top floor. You say that corporal was out on the town, so that leaves him clear. Forgetting the string and pin angle, that is."

"With him you can forget it," I assured him. "That boy was in no condition to tie a pin to a piece of string for twenty-four hours before or after."

"You figure there is any chance of an angle on this Major Harrison? Maybe he figured the Colonel was a disgrace to the military profession."

I crossed the room and brought back the beer. "Go ahead," I told him. "We don't seem to be doing any better without this stuff." He poured himself a bottle without arguing.

"What about this Mr. and Mrs. Campbell?" Charley wondered. "Maybe he seduced this daughter of theirs. Or maybe they had an older daughter he seduced ten years ago."

Even without the beer, I couldn't have denied that the Colonel was a disgrace to the military profession or that he might have seduced one or both of the Campbell's daughters. Or anybody else's daughter, for that matter.

"How do you ring Bronson and the La Tour girl in?" I wanted to know.

"Maybe that's not the real Bronson. Maybe they knocked him off and planted some gunman in his place, with the La Tour girl to give him an alibi." Charley took a long swallow of beer and began to get enthusiastic. "We could send a picture of this guy back to Chicago and see if he is a ringer or not."

"Sure, sure. And we could have men tracing the past history of La Tour and Campbell and Barlow. Have you got any idea what that would cost? Or any idea what Watson would say about it?"

He hadn't had enough beer not to know what Watson would say about it. He shuddered at the thought. But what else was there to do? He wanted to know.

"Think, man, think. Maybe we can get somewhere by pure detection. Forget the evidence and tell me what you really think happened. Then maybe we can prove it."

"I think he shot himself," Charley said promptly. "I think you want to hang around this town for a while and this seems like a good excuse to do it."

That was bad, not so much because I put too much store in Charley's theories as because it was a pretty fair indication of the way it was probably looking to Watson. Unless some evidence happened along soon to upset that suicide theory, I could see us being hauled off the case. The trouble was that the only way I could think of to go after that evidence didn't appeal too much to me.

"Would you believe it wasn't suicide if I prowl around acting like I'm digging up something, and somebody tries to knock me off?"

Charley looked interested, and considerably more sober. He said that if I really meant it he would stick around and be the first to get the man who finished me. Then, he said, we would have something to go on.

"You mean you would have something to go on. I wouldn't be much interested. I've got enough guys following me around waiting to nail the philanthropist who shoots me. I want somebody that shows more concern about stopping it a little sooner."

We discussed ways and means of putting on my clay pigeon act. It was then about four in the afternoon, which seemed too early for manslaughter. I told Charley to see what he could do about digging up a line on Briggs, or at least getting his prints so we could have them checked. Meantime I would prospect around a bit on my own, while it was daylight and presumably safe.

Charley wasn't enthusiastic about the Briggs assignment. He said:

"I hate getting thrown out of those high class places. Makes a man feel like a tramp. Why didn't you collect a sample of his prints while you were there?" The episode of the cocktail glass was one I had neglected to mention.

"I didn't think about it at the time. Be a magazine salesman or something. It should be a snap."

We arranged for Charley to come to my hotel room at seven o'clock. "Be sure and walk upstairs," I told him, "so that nobody spots you as being with me." His outraged complaints over walking up seven flights of stairs followed me down the hall.

When I entered the lobby of my hotel, I saw Edgar on a sofa over by the desk, his usually placid face a study in irritation. That was about as I expected. More of a surprise was Sergeant Thomas sitting beside him with no expression at all. They got up and followed me into the elevator without saying a word. The elevator girl gave me a long and lingering look, warm as a summer sun. Then in an iceberg tone she asked the cops what floor they wanted.

I unlocked the door and we filed into the sitting room. Silently I offered them the box containing the last of the Colonel's cigars, which Thomas started to refuse until he saw the brand name and changed his mind. Edgar's mouth hung slightly open with surprise, but he accepted too. I held up the Colonel's bottle of Scotch, which had about three shots left, so that they could read the label. Thomas grinned faintly as he nodded.

"Now, look," I said when the glasses were poured. "There's no call for you to act like this. You were pulling a fast one trailing me like that, and I pulled one myself. So we're even."

Thomas took a swallow and puffed appreciatively on the cigar. "Nice smoke," he admitted grudgingly. "You know, there can be serious charges thrown at a fellow who interferes with the performance of an officer's duty."

"Duty, my eye. You've got no right to be trailing me. And I've got a perfect right to shake you if I can. You don't have any charge on me."

"Except stealing a car," Edgar said mildly. The mildness didn't hide the fact that he was mad.

"There is that, of course," I admitted. "But wouldn't you look a little silly dragging me up on a charge like that?" I wasn't as happy about it as I sounded, having counted heavily on Edgar's reluctance to ever let Thomas know it had happened.

"It might embarrass Edgar some, but that isn't what kept me from sending out an alarm for you. The fact is, Marks, I figured you on the level, even if mistaken. You really think someone fogged the old man, and

I'm not anxious for you to get the idea I'm trying to cover up a killing. But having you run around loose like this I won't stand. One more play that gives me half an excuse and I pull you in."

"Why shouldn't I run around loose? I'm a citizen and a taxpayer, you know. The theory is that I've got some rights."

"You may be a taxpayer," he agreed, "but the only right you have in this town is not to ruin its fair name by getting yourself killed here."

"And maybe give you another suicide a little hard to explain. How do you figure I'm in any danger if I'm not on the trail of anything?"

"You are fooling around with a couple of hard characters in Lucky Hart and Roscoe Aims. Blunder around their trails enough and you won't have much trouble picking up something that might make them mad."

"How about your sacred cow, Caldwell? You think I might pick up something that would make him mad?"

Thomas' voice hardened a shade. "The worst you can do with Mr. Caldwell is irritate him, but from my standpoint that's not good. So I'm telling you, one more fast move like today and you get yourself arrested for stealing an automobile and anything else that occurs to me between now and then."

"Okay," I agreed. "Now tell me. What really made you come up here instead of sending for me? I'll never believe that cops in this town are that much different from any others, college education or not."

"Two reasons. One, I wanted to see you as quickly as I could. Two, I wanted to find out what you did this afternoon. Tactfully," he added with a faint grin.

"I appreciate it," I assured him. "I didn't do anything. Just got tired of Edgar's company and went to a movie."

Thomas got up and reached for his hat. "Thanks for the drink," he said. "I'm afraid I classify that as a fast move. Come along. It looks to me like you stole a car."

He meant it. I balanced the inconvenience of going to jail for maybe overnight against Charley's freedom of movement. Charley would probably have to come out in the open to bail me out.

"Sit down," I said wearily, "and I'll tell you about it. But when those cigars are gone you can smoke your own."

We went over the story of the shooting in Frisco, with the same speculation as to the present identities of the parties. Thomas wasn't impressed. He freely admitted the possibility, but couldn't see that it led anywhere. He argued that even though Caldwell were the ex-partner of the Colonel and had run away with the Colonel's wife and daughter, it all added up to even stronger evidence of suicide than before. The Colonel had tried to make a touch, failed, and then shot himself.

"You've dreamed up a possible motive," he admitted. "Allowing for a lot of guesses being facts, that is. But you still fall down on the opportunity. Give me circumstantial or any other kind of evidence on Caldwell, or even show me how he or anyone else could have killed him, and I'll buy it. I'll trace Smallwood's past back to the San Francisco quake. But until you show me a way it could be done, no."

We were interrupted by a knock, and when I opened the door Charley came in, walking as though his feet hurt him. He had the faint beginning of a black eye, and he looked mad. He sat down on a chair by the door and took off his shoes before he said a word.

"I kill myself walking up seven flights of stairs," he said bitterly, "just to keep anybody from knowing I'm working with you, and you sit here with half the police force having a party." He had picked out Thomas and Edgar from my description without any trouble.

"Where did you get that eye?" Thomas wanted to know.

"I had an argument with a magazine salesman."

I told Charley that Thomas and I had agreed to level with each other, and explained that Charley had gone out to try to pick up Briggs' fingerprints. Without much luck, apparently. Charley refused to talk about the fingerprint incident. Then he brightened up and said that while he hadn't gotten the fingerprints, he knew Briggs' record anyway.

"I decided to quit doing it the hard way, in spite of the master mind," he said, with a nasty look at me. "I looked him up in the police files. You've got an obliging man on duty there, Sergeant. Briggs has served time twice for armed robbery and once for manslaughter, but he isn't wanted anywhere now."

Thomas and I looked at each other. "How did you know what name to look under?" he asked in a strangled voice.

Charley appeared surprised. "Under Briggs, of course. Ain't that his name?"

Thomas got up abruptly and said that he had things to attend to. "Come on, Edgar," he said. "And no more riding around with these characters either. Tail them like you're supposed to. I don't want you to get the reputation of being friendly with undesirable citizens." Edgar winked at me as they went out.

Charley and I ordered beer sent up and then sat batting the case around for awhile, not coming to any particularly brilliant conclusion. Charley obviously thought the Colonel had probably shot himself, but he didn't make any special point of it. He didn't figure that was his business. If I wanted him there to work on an imaginary murder, that was all right with him. Suddenly he reached in his pocket and took out a length of fishing line and a paper of straight pins. Also a half-dozen safety pins of assorted sizes.

"I'm getting sick of all this talk about pins and strings," he explained. "Let's give it a whirl."

We had polished off a couple more beers apiece, and it struck me as a logical development. We argued briefly about whether to use the straight pins or the safeties, and ended by taking them both outside to the stair door. Half an hour later we had come to no conclusion except that while there might be people who could foil the lock with that apparatus, Charley and I weren't among them. And by that time the fine edge of enthusiasm engendered by the beer had worn off, and I remembered that the idea had started as a gag and that it belonged strictly on that plane.

As we gathered up our equipment, the elevator door opened without warning, discharging the erstwhile drunken Corporal Stevens. Charley was still on his hands and knees on the floor, looking for a pin he had dropped. The elevator girl took a look at us and seemed more than somewhat surprised, for which I didn't blame her.

The corporal gave us the cold, superior look of a man who happens to be sober at the moment, dealing with those who aren't. We went our separate ways with no comments exchanged, although the elevator girl gave me a brief and fairly promising smile.

Inside the suite, I looked up the Caldwells in the phone book and dialed their number. The gravel voice that answered obviously belonged to Briggs. I asked for Miss Caldwell. Sounding about as gracious as a traffic policeman, but not suspicious, he agreed to call her.

When she picked up the phone, she seemed reasonably glad to hear from me, which was pleasant and something of a surprise. She readily agreed to go out to dinner on such short notice. I declined her offer to pick me up at the hotel, saying that I had a car and would drop by for her.

Charley was looking disapproving when I hung up. "Why don't you use her car?" he demanded. "You could have put the rental on the expense account anyhow."

That was a good point, one I had already thought of and discarded because I wanted her family to know for sure whom she was with. I told Charley I didn't believe in chiseling on expense accounts.

We agreed on a program for the evening. We would both rent cars, and Charley would stick to me like glue throughout the evening. He asked where I wanted him in the procession in relation to Edgar and such other parties as might be following along. I told him to bring up the tail of the parade to see what he could get a line on. He departed for his seven flight trek, grumbling.

CHAPTER FIFTEEN

AT THE drive-it-yourself garage I picked out a nearly new Ford convertible that looked as though it could get out and move if the occasion demanded. Charley, in a '47 gray Plymouth, tagged along several blocks behind me, giving Edgar a chance to pull in between us, but as nearly as I could tell no one else was interested in the convertible.

I parked in the Caldwell driveway, with Edgar about a block up the street. Charley wasn't in sight. As I reached for the knocker, the door opened and there stood Briggs, wearing a look that made yesterday's welcome seem prodigal. Before he could say anything, I told him I had an appointment with Miss Caldwell. His look plainly doubted it, but he did let me in and jerked his thumb at a chair in the entrance hall. The idea seemed to be that I could stay there while he talked it over with someone.

He hadn't been gone thirty seconds when Thornton Caldwell came into the hall. Caldwell didn't look as politely disinterested as at the time of my last call. In fact, he appeared to be, in a quiet and restrained way, killing mad. Which of course could have been caused either by a fear of my finding out something about him or a natural distaste for having his daughter annoyed by a detective.

"This seems to call for an explanation of some sort, Marks," he said. "Just what interest do you have in my daughter?" Briggs stood just behind him and to the side, his hands in his pockets.

Fortunately Tony Caldwell wasn't a girl who keeps you waiting. She came down the stairs in time to hear her father's remark.

"What calls for an explanation?" she demanded. "Is it so amazing for a man to ask me out to dinner?"

Caldwell didn't like her being there. He apparently wasn't accustomed to playing the heavy father, and he didn't want to explain whatever was worrying him. He frowned uncertainly at her before he answered. "This man is a detective, Antonia. This is a trick of some sort. I would prefer that you not go with him."

She laughed. "I don't think he would waste his time as a detective on me, Dad. I don't know anything that would be in the least interesting to him. I think he just wants to take me out to dinner."

They argued about it briefly in a circumspect sort of way while I acted embarrassed and Briggs watched me hungrily. Eventually Tony and I found ourselves outside in the convertible, alone, if you could call anyone alone with a cavalcade of that size following.

"I'm sorry about that," she said. "Dad is awfully jumpy since he has been having these labor troubles. He sees kidnappers behind every bush where I'm concerned."

I told her I didn't blame him, and asked where she wanted to eat. She said that it made no difference, and agreed when I suggested a drive to a spot out on the highway. I gathered that her annoyance with Tom Pierce continued. She said he was playing handball that night.

Tony Caldwell was not only beautiful; she was a nice girl, a girl it would be fun to be with sometime when my mind didn't have to be so much on business. She didn't ask me to confirm or deny her father's suspicions — just accepted the fact that it was a casual dinner date, and seemed to be enjoying it. We talked a little bit, mostly about my imaginary boyhood adventures that had influenced me to become a detective. I said I supposed she had been born with a silver spoon in her mouth. She laughed and spoke about her own childhood, and as far as I could tell she, at least, thought she had been born with that spoon. She said Briggs had been with them about five years, appearing to regard him as a harmless eccentricity of her father's.

We stopped at a place on the highway which she recommended. It was a long, low building that combined rough log walls and an elaborate neon sign. Inside, there was a bar along the front, presided over by two inconspicuous bartenders, while the rest of the room was given over to small tables with red-checked covers. A narrow strip down the center was given over to dancing. Nothing about the place looked suspicious to me.

Tony didn't want a drink. She claimed she was ravenous, and had suggested this place because they specialized in fried chicken which was out of this world.

We selected a table about halfway along the back wall, where we could see the bar as well as the rest of the dining room. It was early yet, without much of a crowd at the tables and only a few people at the bar. Edgar settled himself alone at a table near the front. There was no sign of Charley, but I was confident that he was in some spot outside where he had a good view through the windows.

A waitress took our order, and we danced while we waited for the chicken. I found that I still liked dancing with Tony. She seemed to enjoy it, too. I was sorry to see the waitress stop at our table with our orders.

Tony devoured her chicken with as much gusto as Vera or Mabel would have shown. A million dollars certainly didn't affect her appetite. I saw Charley wander in and climb on a stool at the bar. This was shaping up as the kind of an assignment that Charley really loved.

We danced again when we finished eating, then sat at the table and talked. Not about anything in particular, most of the time. I brought up the subject of the Colonel, saying that I had seen her drop him off at the hotel. She appeared genuinely surprised to hear that he was dead, showing no more shock than was to be expected of a casual acquaintance. The papers hadn't given it much of a play, and it was possible that she hadn't read an account of the suicide. If she was putting on an act, it was exceedingly well done.

"How did you happen to be driving him?" I asked.

"Dad asked me to. They had been talking about stock or something. He seemed an awfully nice old fellow — sort of pathetic, somehow." Suddenly she looked at me intently. "Jonny, is that why we are here — why you're interested in me? Something about that old man's death?"

I should have denied it. It would have been possible to work up a story that would satisfy her, and I should have done it. Instead, I told her the truth; that I was investigating the Colonel's death, and wanted to know if she had any information about his relationship with her father. She didn't like it, of course. She was hurt, and the warm friendly atmosphere wasn't there any more. But she didn't look in the least frightened.

It was, surprisingly to me, about eleven o'clock by that time. I didn't know where the time had gone. Until then it had been that kind of an evening. Edgar had stayed at his table all through the evening. Charley had drunk for a time at the bar, gone to a table and had his dinner, then returned to the bar. I had noticed him in earnest conversation with another lone bar-fly, a medium-sized, sandy-haired young fellow wearing a brown gabardine suit.

When I glanced up this time, Charley was by himself. I saw him sway a bit on the stool, try to get up, then fall forward on his face. Drunk or sober, Charley didn't fall down, and when working on a case Charley didn't get really drunk. My nerves jumped like an aching tooth.

I shot a glance at Edgar, saw that he was watching the bar and was starting to get out of his chair. There was a man standing just behind him, but I didn't get a good look at him before I saw the fellow in the brown suit, the one who had been talking to Charley, strolling towards us, hands in pockets. He was still about three tables away.

There wasn't time to get Tony away, there wasn't time to do much of anything. I brushed a fork to the floor with my elbow, and bent over to pick it up. When I straightened up, the Mauser was cradled in my hand, hidden by the edge of the tablecloth. And the brown suit was standing by our table with his pocket pointing toward me in a casual sort of way. Such of the other customers as were paying attention to anything but themselves were watching the bar, where a couple of waiters were trying to get Charley on his feet.

"If the young lady will excuse us, Mr. Marks, we might step outside for a few minutes' chat," Brown Suit said pleasantly. He had a mild, soft voice with no edge to it. He was about twenty-five, and looked about as tough as the average drug store clerk. I didn't want to make any mistake.

"You'll have to show it to me," I said. "No bluffs for me tonight." I hooked the toe of my shoe around one leg of Tony's chair.

"Sure, if that's the way you want it. No sudden moves with those hands, now." He turned slightly sideways and raised his right hand just enough so that I could see the butt of an automatic. There was no change in the texture of his voice.

I make no claim to be a hero, but I knew that once on my feet and with my hands empty, I was gone. There could be but one thing he wanted to talk to me about like that. This was my chance, such as it was. I knew I could get him. Whether or not he got me too depended entirely on how quick his reflexes were.

"All right," I said, "take it easy. That convinces me." I tried to sound scared, which wasn't so hard. Then I did three things all at once. I pulled the trigger of the Mauser, yanked the leg of Tony's chair so that she fell backward out of the line of fire, and threw myself back and to the side. His shot sounded just after mine. I lit rolling and twisted around the corner of the table where I could throw down on him again from the floor.

I didn't shoot. He stood there looking surprised, the automatic slack in his hand. As nearly as you can aim in such a situation, I had tried to go for his shoulder, to leave him in a talking condition, but I hadn't dared to cut it so fine that I might miss. One glance was enough to see that the slug had caught him too low and too close in. A Mauser .25 doesn't knock a man over backwards like a .45, but in the right spot it will do the business. I knew he was gone before he slumped to the floor.

Crowds are funny at a time like that. If any one of them had yelled, they would all have been screaming; if one had moved, they would all have been milling around. This time nobody started it, and the only movement or sound in the place was made by the man who had been standing behind Edgar. He was lunging for the door. The gun in his hand set him sufficiently apart from the herd to keep them from joining in.

I started up the room after him, not daring to shoot because of the crowd. He turned at the doorway, saw me coming, and threw one wild shot in my general direction before he ran outside. Just before I reached the door a voice outside yelled something, there was a flurry of shots close together, then dead quiet. I wasn't too happy going through that door.

Outside, the parking area was well lit by flood lights. My man was lying on his face about a dozen feet from the building. A chocolate-brown young fellow with a police positive in his right hand was climbing out of a 1941 Cadillac convertible. He held up his left hand to me to let the light shine on the badge cupped there.

"You must be Mr. Marks," he remarked quietly, showing no excitement. "I'm Willie Smith."

I don't know why I was so surprised. After all, Edgar had told me. I just never happened to meet a colored homicide man before.

The inside of the restaurant was becoming a screaming madhouse. Smith had the presence of mind to step swiftly to the door, flashing his badge in the faces of the first group that tried to come boiling out, to prevent the crowd from engulfing the man on the ground. They halted at his command, but the maneuver was nullified by the group that came out one of the side doors and swirled around the parking area. I will say they at least gave the body on the ground a wide berth. I took a quick look and satisfied myself that it was just that, a body.

I cut around the building to re-enter by the side door and found Tony still standing by our table, wide-eyed and scared but apparently unhurt. Either my imagination was playing tricks or she was extremely glad to see me come back.

"Are you okay?" I asked. She nodded. "Slip out this door and go sit in the car. Try to get down so no one notices you. I'll be out as soon as I take a look at a couple of friends, and I'll try to get you away before the reporters spot you." Then a thought came to me which I should have had before. "Or would you prefer to have the police or someone else take you home? I wouldn't blame you a bit."

She shivered and moved closer to me for a moment. "I'd rather go with you," she said, and went swiftly outside. I was positive that she was entirely safe, but she didn't know that, and it took nerve to go out alone into the dark.

I could hear Willie Smith outside trying to create some semblance of order out of the crowd, which by this time had emptied the building. Cars were being driven away in spite of his efforts to stop them. It's quite a trick for one man to handle a mob like that and I wasn't critical of Willie for not having the knack, since I certainly don't have it myself. They would probably have knocked me down at the door.

An excited fat man whom I took to be the proprietor was yelling into the telephone in two languages for the police. One of the bartenders was hauling Charlie to a sitting position on the floor. I knelt beside him, found his pulse and watched him breathe, and came to the conclusion that he wasn't dead and gave no particular sign of dying.

Making the rounds, I went to take a look at Edgar. He lay collapsed across his table with an ugly gash in the back of his head. He was breathing, too. I felt his pulse, deciding to find out some day just how fast a pulse should be so it would mean something to me. He looked to me to be in worse shape than Charley.

A fellow who said he was a doctor came bustling in. He had been around the place for several hours, partying with a group several tables from ours. Before the disturbance I would have made the off-hand observation that he was drunk. He seemed all right now, quite steady of hand as he bent over Edgar, but I still wouldn't have wanted to have him fooling around my own cracked head. However, I hesitated to stop him, since he undoubtedly knew more about it in any condition than I did cold sober. I went back to where the bartender was trying to force a drink of something down Charley's throat.

"Looks like he's had a mickey," the bartender told me.

"Who served him besides you?" I asked, flashing my credentials at him. I pulled Charley's .32 out of the waistband of his pants and put it in my own pocket.

He gave me a tired look, somewhat less than scared to death. "Nobody but me. Jack was working the other end of the bar. This fellow was talking to a dozen guys here tonight. Anybody could have slipped him the business."

A siren began to scream far down the highway. The thought of Tony Caldwell shivering fearfully out in the car nagged at me. "Think it will hurt him to be moved?" I asked. I was as willing to take a gamble on the bartender's judgment of something which seemed to be his specialty as on that doctor's.

"No," he said. "He's sleeping like a baby."

"Help me get him to the car," I requested.

Willie Smith came in as we carried Charley between us toward the door. Willie looked mad, frustrated and just a little as though he were going to be sick. I knew how he felt. Shooting a man is nothing you walk away from and forget.

"Okay for me to take the girl out of this?" I asked, jerking my head toward the car. He nodded absently, his eyes searching the place. "Edgar is over there, with a recent drunk who says he is a doctor. Crack on the head. You better keep an eye on them."

As we went on to the car, I told myself that the Caldwell name was certainly a power in that town. No other key would have let two participants in a double shooting walk away from the scene like that. While we loaded Charley into the back seat of the convertible, a state patrol car came howling into the parking area. One of the troopers jumped out and rushed inside, while the other joined the group around the body. We drove away without comment or interference from anyone.

Tony took one quick look in the back seat and huddled tightly against me. "He's not dead," I assured her. Charley gave a monumental snore which added its reassuring note.

The ride home was a silent one. Tony wasn't hysterical, as most girls would have been, but she was far from being so stoic as not to be upset. I owed her an explanation and hoped that by the time she was able to listen there would be an acceptable one I could give her. Meantime it was a comfort that she didn't seem to be blaming me.

It was only a little after twelve when we pulled into the Caldwell driveway.

I helped Tony out and we walked up the driveway without saying a word.

Thornton Caldwell opened the door before we reached it. Tony's composure broke then as she threw her arms around his neck and began to cry. Caldwell not unnaturally gave me a long hard look over her shoulder.

"Well, Marks, what is this? What have you done?" His tone matched his look. It wasn't hard to imagine him a killer just then.

Tony lifted her cheek from his shoulder. Her voice was under good control.

"Jonny hasn't done anything. Not to me. But a man tried to shoot us and Jonny shot him and another man was shot and . . ." She was close to collapse.

Caldwell's face was sinister as she finished. "I'll see you tomorrow, Marks," he said, dismissing me. "I want to look after this girl now." I found myself outside without further discussion. That was all right, as I had my own baby to look after.

Charley was breathing regularly, snoring occasionally, and seemed quite comfortable. I stopped worrying about him and began to think of the advice I would give him on how to be a bodyguard when he snapped out of it.

I nosed the convertible into the hotel's passenger loading zone and leaned on the horn. Jerry eventually came out to the car. "Do you work twenty-four hours a day?" I asked.

He took a look in the back seat before answering. "Man," he said, "is he out like a light. Naw, I'm just swapping shifts with a guy. Where do you want to put this tank?" I wasn't sure whether he meant Charley or the car.

"My friend is sick. Help me up to the room with him."

"Not as sick as he's going to be," Jerry said. We both took hold of Charley, who breathed heavily and helped us not at all. "I'll say this for him though — he's a quiet drunk. Vera says you get nasty." We walked

Charley between us through the lobby and into the elevator.

I told the desk clerk in passing to call a doctor right away. He raised an eyebrow but indicated that he would go along with the gag. The night elevator girl stared at us frankly as we rode upstairs.

After depositing Charley on one of the beds, I gave Jerry a dollar and told him to put the car in the hotel garage. "And I looked at the mileage before I got out," I told him. His attempted look of injured innocence didn't quite come off.

The doctor who came about thirty minutes later was undeniably sober. He was also mad as soon as he took one look at Charley. He listened to my explanation but obviously remained convinced that he had been dragged out in the middle of the night to minister to a drunk. After the examination, he concluded that there was nothing wrong with Charley that sleep wouldn't cure, so his fee seemed ten dollars well spent. I took Charley's shoes off and went to bed myself.

CHAPTER SIXTEEN

THE TELEPHONE bell waked me with an insistent jangling. My watch showed just five minutes to eight as I took the receiver off the hook. Thomas' voice barked at me before I got the first "hello" half out.

"I'm picking you up at the curb in front of your hotel in ten minutes. And I mean ten minutes, without waiting for you to shave or eat if you haven't already. This is hot." He banged down the receiver without waiting for an answer. It was the first time I had ever heard him really excited.

Charley was sleeping in apparent peace and comfort in the adjoining twin bed. I planted a reasonably light kick as I swung my feet over the side. He sat up immediately, instantly awake and alert without preamble. His glance flicked quickly around the room before he closed both eyes tight and shuddered painfully.

"I don't feel so good," he said simply, and probably with some understatement.

He started dressing rapidly enough when I repeated Thomas' short conversation, although he kept his eyes closed when not actually searching for a garment. I gained on him there and so had time to run the electric razor over my face quickly before he finished tying his necktie. He looked awful.

We got to the sidewalk within ten minutes, just in time to see a black Buick come around the corner with its siren howling and pull up just in front of us. Thomas was alone in the back behind the uniformed driver. We climbed into the back seat at the jerk of his thumb and the Buick screamed off up the avenue. Charley sat huddled in the corner with his head clutched in his hands.

Thomas had his excitement under control by this time. His tone was merely conversational as he told me the two gunmen who had jumped me the night before had been identified. Not that I had been interested enough to even stick around and ask him, he pointed out.

"We were sleepy," I said irritably. "And tired of being shot at. All right, I'll bite. Who were they?" The car took a corner on two wheels about then, throwing me against Charley and earning me a short but earnest cursing.

"A couple of night-watchmen from one of Caldwell's local plants." It seemed to me that Thomas was watching me with exaggerated interest as he said it.

"Well, by God, that should do it. Now maybe you'll show a little interest in Caldwell's activities." For the first time I noticed that we were tearing along in the general direction of the Caldwell house. "Don't tell me you're going to break down and ask the great man himself what gives?"

"I'll show a little interest, but I'm not going to ask him anything. That's what this trip is about. Caldwell is dead."

I've never prided myself particularly on being a poker-faced character, and especially at that moment there seemed to be no harm in letting him know how surprised I was. If half of what I felt showed, it should have dissipated any theory he might have held as to my having had a hand in it. Even Charley raised his head and briefly opened his eyes.

"All right, you've had your fun," I said finally. "Are you going to tell me about it?"

"I don't know anything about it. I just got the call from a cruising radio car before I called you. They're out at the house. I thought you might like to ride along."

I was certainly glad to go along, whatever his reasons for picking me up might have been. The news of Caldwell's death had tossed a bombshell into the tentative theory I had begun to spin about the previous events. The identity of the gunmen had seemed to further that theory. This development did it no good. It made it so silly, in fact, that I was glad Charley had been in no condition to listen to me expound.

"How's Edgar getting along?" I asked.

"He'll live. Even if he doesn't get promoted. At that, he seems to have done as well as your own imported bodyguard."

The baffled look which shared the anguish on Charley's face as we both turned our attention to him reminded me that he was still in complete ignorance of everything that had happened since he slid off his bar stool the night before. However, we pulled up to the Caldwell house just then, stopping with a lurch behind a radio car parked at the curb.

Thomas leaped out and headed for the door. Following at his heels, I looked around from a point halfway up the walk to see Charley leaning against the fender and being very sick on the sidewalk. The driver, from solicitude either for Charley or the car, was trying to hold his head. That seemed about all that anyone could do, so I followed Thomas into the house.

The uniformed cop standing inside the front door filled the role of butler about as convincingly as Briggs did. He was big, beefy and dumb-looking. He jerked his thumb at the stairway. "The stiff's upstairs," he said. "Steve is with him."

Thomas paused in his rush for the stairs. "Now that's brilliant. Four months on the force, and he's up at the scene while you're down here.

What's the idea?"

"I figured this was the best spot to keep an eye on everything. All he's got to do is not touch anything, and don't worry, he's not going to do that."

"Where's all the family?"

The cop reddened a little, though not much. "Upstairs," he admitted.

Thomas went on upstairs without saying anything more. I gathered from his red neck and ears that he was mad, and I put the silence down to iron self-control or a knowledge that a homicide sergeant hasn't much command over radio car patrolmen anyhow. Probably the latter. Myself, I didn't blame the guy much. I'm not fond of sitting around with dead bodies either, and what is the good of seniority if you can't pull it at a time like that?

Briggs was waiting in the upper hall, just outside Caldwell's study door. He looked meaner than ever, if possible, and also vaguely unhappy.

"What are you doing out here?" Thomas barked at him, somewhat unreasonably, I thought. Still, it was as good an opening as any. Briggs didn't appear too sensitive.

"Where else?" he asked. "The mug downstairs chases me up here, and the punk in there," jerking his head at the study door, "chases me out of that room."

"Where's the family?" Thomas demanded, ignoring the explanation. He probably hadn't thought much of the question himself.

"Mrs. Caldwell is in her room, crying. The kid is with her. And the cook is down in the kitchen crying."

Thomas grunted and opened the study door. "Stay there," he told Briggs as we went in. Briggs sneered at him without exactly changing the expression on his face. That sounds like quite a trick, but Briggs could do it.

The study wasn't as attractive as the last time I had been there. A corpse sprawled across a desk can ruin a room's appeal, somehow. The young cop, Steve, over by the window, obviously thought so too. He kept his eyes fixed on us, avoiding the body. Steve had an intelligent, pugnacious face and square husky shoulders that had probably filled a college football jersey not too long before. At the moment his complexion was a pasty gray.

"Everything in order, Sergeant," he said in a strained voice, and swallowed carefully.

"Okay," Thomas said. He looked sharply at the kid and added: "Go on downstairs and have Calkins report to me."

Steve said, "Yes, sir," and headed gratefully for the door.

Thomas eyed me for a moment as though waiting for a crack. "Don't glare at me," I told him. "I'm throwing no stones. You should have seen me with my first stiff. Although why 'Everything in order, Sergeant' happened to be the first thing that occurred to him I'll never know."

"Maybe I shouldn't have sent him downstairs, at that. If he sees that man of yours going through his performance, he's a goner, sure." That put him one up. I hadn't realized he had even noticed Charley.

We walked over to the desk and inspected the body. Caldwell wasn't nearly as dignified and austere as the last time I had seen him. One dead man looks about like any other. He was on his face across the desk, arms flung out wide, a pearl-handled .32 revolver lying loosely in the grip of his right hand. There was quite a mess around his right temple, with blood spreading out over the desk. It had every appearance of suicide, certainly. I didn't look very long myself.

The rest of the room was in perfect order. The ash tray on the desk had half a dozen cigarette ends in it — otherwise the place was immaculate. Thomas grunted irritably and reached for his pipe. Then he glanced back to the desk and put the pipe away. Calkins came clumping in.

"You through with us?" he asked. He didn't look at the body, either.

"I'll tell you when I'm through," Thomas snapped at him. "Give me your report."

"Nothing to report. Call came over the radio there was a dead man here. We were over at Tenth and Adams and we got here in five minutes. That guy out in the hall met me at the door. He brought us up here, and there was the stiff. I looked around up here — nobody here but a couple of dames sniveling in one of the bedrooms. Nobody downstairs except a dame sniveling in the kitchen. Then you got here — we only beat you by about twenty minutes."

"That's a brilliant piece of work," Thomas said, still unreasonable.

"Thanks." Calkins got the idea across that to him homicide sergeants were a dime a dozen. "What's eating you? So a rich guy shoots himself. Can you figure a way to get your name in the paper on that?" I gathered that there was some dissension in the local police department.

"Stay here and don't touch anything until the fingerprint squad shows up." Thomas motioned to me and went out into the hall, leaving Calkins there alone. The sergeant had the last word on that one, all right.

"I want a room I can talk to you people in, one at a time," Thomas told the waiting Briggs. "What's the best bet?"

Briggs' answer was almost polite. "Downstairs, I guess. But do you need to bother the women, Sarge? They're all busted up." He started down the stairs, and took us into the big room that opened off the hall.

Thomas chose a big chair by the fireplace and hauled a notebook out of his pocket. "Sit down," he told Briggs. "I want to talk to you first."

Briggs looked even more sinister as he said: "Not for a couple of minutes.

I'll be back."

"You'll be back nothing. I said sit down."

"I got to go to the bathroom."

Thomas glared at him as though suspecting a sinister motive, but there is no way to prove a man doesn't need to go to the bathroom. Just then we heard an argument out in the hall, which Thomas seemed to welcome as an excuse to get up and go to the door.

"Let him in," I heard him say. "I need him." He came back, followed by Charley, who was still pale around the gills but in considerably better shape than when I had left him.

"Take this guy to the can," Thomas told Charley, motioning to Briggs.

Briggs appeared ready to choke. "The magazine salesman," he began, then clamped his jaws together.

"He's big enough to go by himself," Charley said irritably. But he went along.

"Aren't you going to have a stenographer take this down?" I asked Thomas, more to fill in an awkward pause than anything else.

"No. Did you ever see a police stenographer outside the commissioner's office that could read his own notes back?" Then he relaxed and grinned. "Besides, nobody can prove what damn fool questions a man asks if they aren't being taken down."

We smoked for a couple of minutes in silence. Thomas was drawn and worried, lacking the calm assurance that had marked his earlier manner.

There was another disturbance at the door as the fingerprint squad arrived. I recognized the morose-looking fingerprint man and his side kick, the uniformed photographer. Thomas started them on the room with the body.

As he returned to the living room, Pete Hansen arrived. He was shaved and carefully dressed in a dark suit which would have been suitable for a funeral. It was plain enough as he came in that he knew something had happened. Thomas jumped him before he could speak.

"What do you know about this?" he demanded.

"Nothing at all. Briggs called and told me Mr. Caldwell was dead and I hurried right over. How did it happen?"

He acted honestly shocked. Thomas stared hard at him as though to convince him that nothing escaped the eyes of the police force. Hansen evidently missed the point, as in the best indignant taxpayer manner he demanded to be allowed to see Mrs. Caldwell.

Thomas, however, insisted that he talk to him first. Hansen accordingly followed us reluctantly to the living room.

"Was it murder or suicide?" he wanted to know.

"How do you know it was either? Why not accidental death?"

"Because Briggs called up and said Mr. Caldwell was dead and he had just called the police. He suggested I get over as soon as possible and hung up. I naturally assumed it was violence of some sort."

Well, that sounded reasonable. Or at least it sounded possible. Thomas told him politely enough the position in which the body was found, and asked if he had ever considered the possibility of Caldwell committing suicide.

"Good God, no. I would think he would be the last man to do that. When I left last night, he seemed in good enough spirits, except for being angry at this fellow Marks here."

It developed that Hansen had come to the house the night before about ten o'clock to go over some business matters. He claimed that this was a fairly usual occurrence. They had worked in the study until I brought Tony home. Hansen remained upstairs, but Caldwell rushed down to the door as soon as he saw my lights reflected on the windows. When he came back upstairs, he was mad at me for having taken Tony to a place where she would be exposed to danger. They had worked for about half an hour longer, and then Hansen had left. He let himself out the front door, Caldwell staying in the study. Briggs had presumably gone to bed long before.

Thomas questioned him as to the business they had discussed. The explanation was complete and seemingly candid, involving the proposed merger of a couple of steamship lines. I didn't understand it myself and doubted that Thomas was getting much more out of it. He finally shut him off by asking about any enemies Caldwell might have had.

"I suppose you might say he had a lot of enemies, in a business way," Hansen told us. "You know the set-up here. The unions wanted him out of the way. But he was just the head of the opposition — his being gone won't stop the opposition and won't affect the fight much. Personally, I can't see them killing him. So far as I know he didn't have any personal enemies, or even any very close acquaintances. He kept pretty much to himself."

"Where does Briggs fit in? Why did he figure he needed a bodyguard?"

"Briggs was just sort of insurance, I guess. He's a tough mug Caldwell picked from out of his plant guard force, to have someone handy around the house in case of trouble. I never knew why Caldwell picked him instead of a more presentable type, but he seemed devoted to the family and the old man just appeared to feel safer having him around."

"Where did he come from before that?"

Hansen said he didn't know, but understood from a word or two Caldwell had dropped that Briggs had been in some trouble he was trying to live down and Caldwell sympathized with him.

He explained his own relationship to the dead man as that of a confidential secretary who had grown through the years to something more. He had come to Caldwell directly upon finishing college and had been taken more and more into his confidence until he was now on the board of directors of several of the Caldwell corporations. He told us that he was now making thirty thousand dollars a year, which he figured he owed entirely to Caldwell, and he appeared to be genuinely grateful and also somewhat worried as to his own future now that Caldwell was gone.

Hansen also told us that he was familiar with the terms of Caldwell's will. He said that he himself got twenty-five thousand, Briggs ten thousand, with the balance to Tony and Mrs. Caldwell in equal parts, without any strings of any sort. All of this information later checked out to be accurate.

Hansen made a good impression during the questioning. He was nervous and upset, but not abnormally so, under the circumstances, and kept fretting about wanting to see Mrs. Caldwell and Tony. He didn't point out that Caldwell's death would be a loss to him — it didn't appear to occur to him that he was a possible suspect. Thomas finally asked him flatly:

"Do you think Caldwell committed suicide?"

"I don't know what to think. I very much doubt it."

"Do you think his wife or daughter killed him?"

"Good God, no. That's utterly ridiculous."

"Do you think Briggs killed him?"

"I don't think so, no. It isn't as preposterous as suggesting Tony or Mrs. Caldwell, but somehow I don't think so."

"Could an outsider have broken in?" Thomas asked. I had been wondering when we would get around to what would have appeared to me to be a fairly routine early step.

"I shouldn't think so, unless a window is broken somewhere. The door was locked when I left, and I know they are careful about locks everywhere in the house."

"You see where that leaves you," Thomas said pleasantly. "You were admittedly the last man to see him alive. You say the others in the house didn't kill him. You don't think an outsider got in. You don't think he committed suicide."

Unexpectedly Hansen laughed. "Then I'm wrong somewhere, because I didn't kill him." His tone got a bit harder. "Put like that, I suppose he must have shot himself. It just surprised me, that's all. Now I'm going up to see if there is anything I can do for Mrs. Caldwell."

This time Thomas didn't attempt to stop him. After he was gone, the Sergeant looked at me and shrugged his shoulders. "It could be," he said.

"He might prefer twenty-five thousand in a lump sum to future prospects."

"He might," I agreed. "Do you really think so?" He admitted that he didn't.

The uniformed driver from Thomas' car came in then. He ignored us while he made a careful inspection of the windows, testing and probing at each one until he was satisfied. We watched silently until he turned to face us.

"Not from outside," he said. "There are shrubs or flower beds under every window that can be opened, and they are all well cultivated. Nobody has walked on them since the last rain. If these windows and doors were left last night like they are now, nobody got in unless they were let in a door or had a key." Thomas nodded to him and he went out.

Thomas grinned sardonically at my expression. "We miss a lot, but not that much," he said. I told him I was glad to see he saved the taxpayers money by combining a chauffeur and a detective, and silently congratulated myself on not having sounded off.

The police doctor arrived and met some criticism from Thomas for having taken so long. The doctor doubted that it made any difference to the patient. We all went upstairs, trailed by Charley and Briggs, who had been waiting in the hall. Thomas made Briggs wait outside while the rest of us went into the study.

The gun had been removed from Caldwell's fingers, presumably for printing, but otherwise nothing had been disturbed. The fingerprint man and the photographer were packing up their stuff. Thomas' driver was poking around at the upholstery of one of the easy chairs.

"Find anything interesting?" Thomas asked.

"Sure," the print man said. "Prints all over the gun. I think they are the stiff's. Sort of smudged, though."

"Like it had been handled afterwards by somebody else?"

"Blamed if I know. I just said they were sort of smudged. I'm no magician."

At times it appeared to me that Thomas carried democracy too far. Myself, I would have knocked a couple of heads together on that police department. They couldn't all be nephews to the commissioner.

The uniformed driver, whom Thomas belatedly introduced as Eric Roberts, said that he had been over the room with a fine-tooth comb and couldn't find anything out of the way. The two technical experts went back to the station to write their reports. Thomas asked the doctor if he thought Caldwell could have committed suicide. The doctor was in a vicious mood himself.

"That's a silly question," he said. "Of course he could have committed suicide. Any time you find a guy with a hole in his head and a gun in his hand, he could have committed suicide. When I dig out the bullet, we'll check to see if it came from this gun. He was shot from close up."

"How long has he been dead?" Thomas asked.

"Quite a while. Several hours." The doctor added that a cursory examination had shown no other signs of violence, but he promised to do a complete post-mortem. He didn't hide his opinion that the whole business was a lot of trouble for a suicide. When he discovered that no one had yet called for the police ambulance, the doctor inquired nastily whether we expected the corpse to walk or him to do the autopsy there. He put in the call and went away.

Thomas called Briggs into the room, showed him the gun, and asked if he recognized it.

"Sure," Briggs told him. "It belongs to Mr. Caldwell. He kept it in the right-hand drawer of the desk there."

"Who knew that?"

"Everybody, I guess. At least I knew it." Briggs sounded pretty subdued, but not particularly scared. He didn't avoid looking at the body and didn't stare at it. To Briggs it seemed to be just a piece of furniture.

Thomas broke the gun and showed me that one chamber was empty, while a second held an exploded cartridge. "Did he carry the hammer on an empty chamber?" he asked Briggs.

"I don't know. I never looked at it specially."

Roberts silently took a box of .32 calibre cartridges out of the drawer and showed them to Thomas. The sergeant stuck them under Briggs' nose. I saw that the box was about half full.

"Any shells missing from this?" Thomas asked.

Briggs said he didn't know. Any other answer would have sounded darned peculiar, unless he had a passion for counting pistol bullets. He said that Caldwell went out to the gun club and shot the pistol at a target once in a while.

Thomas suddenly remembered something else and asked Briggs for his gun. The butler silently hauled a massive Colt .45 automatic from his hip pocket. Thomas unloaded it, smelled it, and peered down the barrel, then tossed it to Roberts.

"You got a permit?" he asked.

"No. I didn't think I needed a permit just to carry it around the house."

A look of almost intelligent interest crossed Charley's face at that answer. I decided to look it up myself sometime. On the face of it it sounded reasonable that maybe you didn't need a permit to carry a concealed weapon around the house. I never did remember to ask Thomas the answer to that one. I doubt if he knew either.

"How come nobody heard the shot?" Thomas changed the subject.

"The room's soundproofed," Briggs explained.

At Thomas' suggestion that we go back down to the living room to continue the questioning, Briggs protested vigorously. He said he hadn't had breakfast, Mrs. and Miss Caldwell hadn't had breakfast, and the cook wasn't likely to cook any breakfast until he went down and made her do it. Charley pointed out that so far as he knew nobody had had any breakfast. Charley looked as though he could use some food. Briggs said that no one was going to question Mrs. Caldwell until she had something to eat.

Thomas gave in, only stipulating that Charley go along to the kitchen while the food was being cooked. So far as I could see the only reason for that was because Charley and Briggs appeared so disgusted with each other's company. After all, Briggs had had the run of the house for quite a while before we came. The sergeant and I went down to the living room.

"How do you figure it, Marks?" he asked wearily, after we settled ourselves in easy chairs. "Honest to God, do you see any chance of anything but suicide?"

"Well, Hansen could have shot him, tucked the gun in his hand, and gone on home. Or Briggs could have sneaked in later and done it. So could his wife or daughter. So could the cook, possibly. A stranger could have come and thrown rocks at his window, and when he went down to let him —"

"Shut up," Thomas said without passion. "We'll run a paraffin test to see if his hand held that gun, of course. Will you give up if it did?"

"Not necessarily. There could have been two shots, the last one with the murderer squeezing off a shot with the gun in Caldwell's hand. That would show powder marks."

"Where did the second bullet go? And don't tell me Roberts missed it — he doesn't miss stuff like that."

"Well," I offered, "he could have fired into a thick book and taken it away with him. Or a sofa pillow. Or he could have opened a window and shot through it, taking a chance on the sound."

Thomas grinned a little at that. He wanted to know if I had ever tried to put a gun in a dead man's hand and aim at a window or anything else. I pointed out that we were only discussing possibilities. I was just as glad when Charley came in to announce that coffee was ready in the kitchen. He said that Briggs was taking a tray upstairs.

The kitchen was big and shiny and smelled wonderful, which description pretty well fitted the cook. She ran much truer to type than Briggs did. She had been crying, but I thought more from a sense of duty than real grief; she seemed relieved to be busy with breakfast. She gave us bacon and eggs and coffee and toast and even offered to make pancakes for us if we wanted them. She was the only one in that town who seemed to have a really proper respect for the police force.

Briggs stayed upstairs for a long time, long enough for us to get a pretty good interview from the cook without making a point of it. We didn't get much. She had been with the family for ten years. She thought Mrs. Caldwell was "wonderful," Tony "sweet," Mr. Caldwell "a fine gentleman and free with money but not a gentleman you got to know well." Briggs, she said with a sniff, at least tried to behave properly around the house. She obviously had dark suspicions as to what he did away from the house.

Briggs slept over the garage in his own apartment. The cook had a room in the basement. There were no other resident servants, as Mrs. Caldwell liked to do some of the housework. A cleaning woman and laundress came in regularly.

Last night the cook had gone to bed early and she had heard nothing until Briggs came down to the kitchen a few minutes before eight to tell her Mr. Caldwell was dead and that he had called the police. She appeared to have every confidence that if anything was wrong the police would straighten it out. I think she irritated Thomas more than anybody else I had seen him interview.

Briggs came back in and drank a cup of coffee while leaning against the sink. His face held an expression that I would have called unhappiness on anybody else. Maybe that is what it was with Briggs. He followed us back to the living room when we were through eating. The cook cordially invited me to send the rest of the boys back for a snack.

The butler insisted that he had gone to bed early in his own apartment over the garage. He swore that he hadn't heard me bring Tony home, hadn't heard Hansen leave, hadn't heard any shots. He went to Caldwell's study at seven-forty-five to straighten the room before Caldwell got up and found the body there. He immediately called the police, then called Hansen.

"Why call him?" Thomas wanted to know.

"The boss trusted him. He handled the boss's business. I figured he would know how to talk to the women."

"What about a doctor? Didn't anybody think to call one?"

Briggs twisted his lips in a way meant for a grin. "You don't need a doctor for a guy in that shape, Sarge."

"You know a lot about guys in that shape, don't you?"

Briggs just sneered at him silently. Thomas changed his challenging tone for a softer approach.

"When did you first meet Caldwell?" he asked.

"I started work as one of his plant guards about ten years ago. He got to talking to me at the gate once or twice, and finally he asked me if I wanted to work here at the house. I said okay, and I been here ever since."

"Ever been in Frisco?" I asked casually.

Briggs may have looked fleetingly ill at ease, or I may have imagined it. "Once or twice," he said. "I been around quite a bit."

"Did you know Caldwell in Frisco?"

"No."

"Did you know a Colonel Smallwood?"

"No."

"Jack Barlow? Captain James?"

"No." He may have been sweating a little, and his voice was even more sullen than usual, but I didn't get the impression that he was approaching the point where he would break down and tell all, if there was anything for him to tell. It is easy to be too harsh in interpreting a man's manner when he is being questioned in a death case. Some of the most innocent ones make the worst showing.

Thomas badgered him for a bit without success. He finally gave up and asked the butler to see if Mrs. Caldwell could talk to us now. Briggs went upstairs without protest.

Mrs. Caldwell came in alone. She had been crying, of course, and her face without makeup was ravaged and haunted. She had herself under control, though. Thomas was gentle and considerate in seating her and trying to put her at ease.

He got nowhere. She was apparently attempting to be co-operative, but she just didn't know anything about it. She and Caldwell slept in separate rooms and so she had no hint of anything wrong until Briggs brought the news to her. Yes, Caldwell often worked late at night. Yes, he trusted Hansen implicitly, almost as one of the family. Briggs was also a trusted employee. Mrs. Caldwell trusted them herself. She knew of no enemies her husband had. She knew nothing of his business affairs. She supposed they were well-to-do, and supposed that most of the money had been left to herself and daughter, but she had never discussed financial affairs with her husband.

There was nothing wrong with her manner that you could put your finger on, her grief seemed deep and perfectly genuine, and yet there was an unease that didn't seem quite called for. She tensed before each question, then relaxed a bit as she answered.

"Mrs. Caldwell," I said suddenly, "may I ask a few questions?" Thomas scowled at me but said nothing. "Sergeant Thomas is in a difficult position," I continued. "He naturally wants to treat you with every consideration. I do, too, of course, and yet there are some things —"

"I intend to see that she is treated with every consideration by all concerned," Thomas cut in. "Don't forget, Marks, you are here on sufferance
from me. I see no justification for submitting Mrs. Caldwell to any sort of
cross-examination."

"I don't intend to cross-examine her," I said gently. "I think it will be
to her advantage to let me say a few words. Then she is at liberty to answer
me or not, as she chooses."

Mrs. Caldwell lifted a slender hand to cut off Thomas' comment. "I'll
be glad to hear what Mr. Marks has to say," she told him. "From what my
daughter tells me I gather that he is a determined, if not a ruthless, young
man. I may as well hear him now."

"Not ruthless where you or your daughter are concerned, Mrs. Caldwell," I said, and meant it. "I'm going to tell you some things which I
believe to be facts. Some of them I can't prove yet. Maybe some of them
I can never prove. It's only fair to tell you, though, that I firmly believe
them, and that all of the very great resources of one of the most reputable
detective agencies in the country will be bent toward verifying those facts.
If it comes to that, it may be impossible to keep them quiet. If you tell us
now, and they prove not to be pertinent to the death of my client, Colonel
Smallwood, they will never be used by me or my agency."

That was quite a speech for me, and not the kind I usually make. Something about the woman, not only the way she met the death of her husband
but the additional tragedy she could sense was coming, got me. Or was I
imagining the whole thing? In another five minutes I would be regarded as
either a smart man or the biggest damned fool on the West Coast.

She looked me steadily in the eye. "I can't imagine what you mean," she
said, "but go on, Mr. Marks."

"I think," I said slowly, "that Thorton Caldwell's real name, or in any
event the name he used in 1927, was Jack Barlow. I think the man I knew
as Alexander Smallwood was known at that time as Captain James. I think
that in San Francisco —"

She stopped me. Not by a word, or a gesture, or much more than a flicker
of expression, but she stopped me. She was ready to talk.

"All right, Mr. Marks," she said quietly, "it's true. All that you are going
to say is true. I was Alec's wife, and Tony is his daughter. I ran away with
Thornton, taking Tony with me, when Alec got in trouble. It wasn't just
that. Thornton and I were both tired of that kind of life, and he was willing
to take me out of it. Alec would never have changed. But I don't suppose
those old reasons matter to you," she said hopelessly, and fell silent.

Thomas took over. He was still considerate and polite, but he wasn't
afraid of her or her influence any more. He had a hold on her that he could

use if he had to. It probably isn't fair to say cops are like that; I suppose anyone is like that under the right set of circumstances.

"What did Smallwood, or James, come to see you about?" he asked.

"He came to blackmail us," she told him. "He was quite frank about it, in flowery language, of course. He said that it had taken him twenty years to trace us, and that now that he had found us it would cost a fortune to keep the scandal out of the newspapers."

"Was there a quarrel?"

"I know this will be difficult to believe, but there was no quarrel at all, even in the beginning. Thornton and I had been half expecting that moment for many years, and were more or less prepared for it. We both knew that we had treated Alec badly, even though no other course seemed open to us at the time. When he finally found us, it was almost a relief."

"How much money did he want?"

"He never did say. In the beginning he was not so blatant as to mention an amount, and in the end money was the farthest from all our thoughts. It was quite an emotional parting."

Thomas rubbed his forehead. "I'm afraid I don't quite understand you, Mrs. Caldwell. What are you trying to tell us?"

"I don't blame you," she said, a hint of a smile showing through her grief. "You would need to know all the participants, particularly Alec, to make this believable. Mr. Marks knew him — he may, perhaps, find it credible.

"I'm trying to say that when Alec saw the life we had built up here, saw that the principal aim in that life was to make Tony happy, saw how Tony felt toward Thornton, he couldn't go through with it. He wasn't a bad man, and he was highly emotional. He also loved to make a grand gesture. He told us finally that he was sorry, that if we would have Tony drive him back to the hotel we would never hear from him again."

"Did you believe him?"

"Yes, I did. It was impossible not to. He was terribly pathetic. He called me that night to say that he was leaving town next morning, and to say good-bye."

"Were you surprised when you heard he had killed himself?"

"In a way, yes. And yet I don't know — he was emotional, and might have felt that there was nothing left in life for him. I felt more grief for him than I ever expected to be able to feel."

"Did you discuss Smallwood's death with Thornton Caldwell?"

"Yes, of course. I believe Thornton was deeply shocked. He had been quite touched by the scene the day before."

"Did you suspect that Mr. Caldwell had any part in Smallwood's death?"

She seemed genuinely surprised. "What can you possibly mean? It was suicide, wasn't it?"

"Yes, I guess it was." Thomas' voice was tired. "Thank you very much, Mrs. Caldwell. I won't need to trouble you further. And don't worry — I don't believe this conversation will need to come out."

"Thank you, thank you both very much. I would like to avoid a scandal for Tony's sake. She has no idea that Thornton is not — was not — her real father."

"Just one or two things more, please," I said. "Who else knows about your background?"

"Briggs does, of course. He worked for Thornton in San Francisco in the old days. They met again several years ago, and Thornton asked him to stay on here. I'm sure he never said anything to anyone. Thornton trusted him."

"Anyone else?"

She hesitated. "I'm just not sure. Pete Hansen might. Sometimes, from things he has said, I have wondered if he might not at least suspect. But no, I'm sure he doesn't. Even though Thornton trusted him almost like a son, I don't believe he would discuss that with him."

Thomas said that he felt he should talk to Tony, just as a matter of form, before leaving. Mrs. Caldwell protested that she was too upset to come down, and asked that it be postponed. They compromised by Thomas agreeing to go up to her room and to be both brief and discreet. I didn't feel that I could face Tony at the moment, so I told Thomas Charley and I would wait for him in the car.

While we sat waiting, I briefed Charley on the events of the night before, starting with the time he passed out. He was bitterly embarrassed about that and unreasonably displeased about the death of the man who had drugged him. His inability to avenge his aching head occupied most of Charley's attention that morning.

By the time Thomas came out, the police ambulance had taken away the body and the radio car was gone. Two reporters had appeared and were dealt with briskly and emphatically by Briggs at the door. They hung around us for a short time, apparently accepting our improbably story that we were friends of Thomas' who happened to be riding along with him and knew nothing about anything. When Thomas came, he told them it was a suicide, no mystery about it. They seemed to accept that, too. They didn't strike me as particularly brilliant newspaper men.

"Sergeant," I said as we drove away, "one thing sort of worries me."

"Just one?"

"At the moment. It's that shooting last night. I know this town is casual about violence, and I know it was self-defense, but isn't somebody going to even talk to me about it?"

"That's a good point," he conceded. "That's something the state patrol boys were a little critical of Willie about, letting you drive away like that. You're lucky, though, that Willie saw the whole thing through the window — he got there early, to relieve Edgar. Edgar was able to talk for a few minutes last night, too. You will have to go down with me to talk to the prosecutor sometime today or tomorrow. This other business sort of pushed it out of my mind."

We rode a few blocks in silence. "What's the next move?" I asked eventually.

"Routine. Check back all we can on those two thugs who tried for you last night. Get the reports on this thing today, though I'm convinced it's suicide. Stuff like that."

"That shooting last night makes it tough for you, doesn't it?" I asked nastily. "If it weren't for that, you could just write off two suicides and move on to the next body."

He really got mad then. "Hang it all," he said, "I'm getting sick of telling you this, Marks, but I'll tell you just once more. Show me how Smallwood could possibly have been murdered and I'll go along with just about any way you say."

"All right," I said, "I'll tell you how he could have been murdered, if you'll give me your word to let me play it my way for twenty-four hours."

He finally agreed to follow any request if my theory on the possible solution was one he could swallow at all. Roberts pulled the car over to the curb while I told them.

Thomas grunted sharply once as he began to get the idea, then listened in complete silence while I finished. Charley had almost a grin on his usually sour face. Roberts swore softly to himself.

"It could be," Thomas finally said. "It certainly could be. On the other hand, it's nothing but a guess."

"Show me any other way it could have been?" I challenged.

"It could have been suicide."

"Then how do you explain the shooting last night, and Caldwell's death?"

He nodded slowly. "Yeah, that's right. But that doesn't mean this hare-brained notion of yours is going to work. If it happened as you say, it's far more likely that Caldwell killed Smallwood, tried to have you killed, then got panicky and shot himself when he thought you were closing in on him. If that's the case, there will be no one to close the trap on."

"Even so, what do you lose trying it my way? If it doesn't work, you can try grilling the suspect we do have alive, you can start tracing back for every possible connection betweeen that party and any of the possibilities, you can do everything you want to do now. If it wasn't Caldwell, my angle might work. Personally, I don't believe it was Caldwell — I can't swallow such a connection between him and our party."

"That's true, sarge," Roberts said. "Lucky Hart would fit that picture much better. Or the house dick — he could have done it. Or Briggs."

"All right," Thomas agreed, "I guess we've got nothing to lose by trying."

"Except Jonny," Charley cut in. "I don't buy it quite the way he lays it out. That deal last night left me looking enough of a fool. If we try this proposition, I'm going to be hiding in the closet. I can't see myself going back to Watson and saying I let him get knocked off on me."

"That's out," I insisted. "That hotel is like a goldfish bowl where you and I are concerned. The way I told you is the only way everybody there will be sure you are out of the picture for the evening. And there's too much danger a cop would be spotted if one tried to hang around. We do it the way I say."

We argued, but they gave in. I would have been glad to try for a safer solution if one had presented itself, since I'm no hero; but a man has his professional pride, and I didn't feel that the Watson agency in general and I in particular had looked brilliant so far. I was anxious to even up the score. Thomas was obviously uneasy about the whole thing. Partly, I thought, for fear that it wouldn't work and partly for fear that it would work and he hadn't thought of such a simple loophole in the first place.

Roberts started up the car and we went back to the hotel without further conversation.

CHAPTER SEVENTEEN

As CHARLEY and I got out of the car in front of the hotel, I slammed the door considerably harder than necessary. "Then the hell with you," I told Thomas.

"I guess he must have told you," Jerry the bellboy said with satisfaction. He had appeared as soon as the car pulled up to the curb.

"You really fixed it up, Sherlock," Charley told me, ignoring Jerry. "If you could keep that imagination of yours in hand, we'd all get along better."

"You can go to hell too," I told him.

Charley left me without saying anything else. He went into the bar which opened off the lobby, leaving me to go on to the elevator alone. Or almost alone. Jerry tagged along as close as a burr.

"How's it coming, Chief?" he wanted to know. "Anything you can use me on?"

He seemed to have lost his suspicions of me and to be casting himself again in the role of a fellow detective.

I pulled him off to one side. "There is something you could do for me," I admitted.

"Do you know any girls who might be free this afternoon?"

He looked disgusted. "I thought you were working on a case. And in the afternoon, too." Then his larcenous nature got the better of him. "Yeah, I might know somebody. I'll give you a call."

At that moment I saw the night elevator girl, Esther Taylor, crossing the lobby.

In uniform she looked to be just a kid, whom I had pictured as a bobby soxer in her off-duty hours, when I thought of her at all. Now she was wearing a blue gabardine suit, high-heeled pumps, stockings so sheer that you had to look twice to be sure she was wearing stockings. That, however, was no hardship. She even wore a hat. The general effect was smart, expensive, and about five years older than in uniform.

"Let it go," I told Jerry. "I've changed my mind."

He had followed my glance. "You're wasting your time," he warned me. "Everybody makes a play for her; nobody gets anywhere."

I left him and crossed the lobby to intercept her. She looked pleased enough when she recognized me.

"How about lunch?" I asked without preamble.

"I'd love to," she said promptly.

I sure was getting irresistible.

I beckoned Jerry over and told him to get the Ford from the parking lot. Esther ignored his leer.

When we were in the car, I asked her where she wanted to eat. She said she didn't care. She didn't add that she wasn't in the habit of going out with strange men from the hotel, but somehow, in a flattering sort of way, she got the idea across to me. Her voice was husky but well-modulated, and she had either been to a careful school or had been raised in a home where that sort of thing was important. Or else she just listened to the radio and had a good ear — I don't pretend that I can ever tell which.

"You name it," I urged. "Some place where we can get a drink and maybe a good steak."

She considered briefly. "I know so little about the habits of detectives, or the sort of places they like to eat."

"Don't believe what you see in the movies," I told her. "Detectives like nice restaurants better than dives, the same as anyone else. Especially when they are out of town and on an expense account."

She named an address and gave me directions to get there. I enjoyed the ride.

She didn't snuggle against me as we rode; in fact, in point of inches she probably sat about where Tony Caldwell had, but the general effect was considerably more intimate. There are times when the life of a detective has its compensations.

We pulled up in front of a dilapidated old house in one of the less attractive parts of town, which was distinguished from other old houses in the area only by a colored canopy stretching from the front door to the sidewalk.

When I looked around for a place to park, she smiled and indicated the uniformed brigadier general type who came out to meet us. That was my first intimation that she had taken me at my word when I told her my expense account made the sky the limit. The stiff-shirted head waiter who met us at the door was another hint.

Opening off one side of the hall of the old-fashioned family residence was a dimly lit dining room. There were half a dozen tables, only one of which was occupied. The room on the other side of the hall had been converted into a bar, with a row of partitioned booths along one wall.

I had seen two waiters in the dining room. In the bar, which we chose, they had a bartender and a male waiter for serving drinks. Then there was the smiling head waiter who showed us in, bowing cordially to Esther. It was altogether too fully staffed not to be either a fine, expensive restaurant which catered to the discriminating gourmet, or else some sort of a clip joint.

No one else was in the bar. The waiter who came to us immediately was an innocuous-looking type, as had been the head waiter. So was the bartender, so far as I could tell. At least there was nothing about their appearance to make me start hollering copper. Nevertheless, we were in a strange city in a joint I didn't know and which I hadn't picked, and I was mixing in a game which had gotten rough at times. I chose a corner booth where I could see most of the room.

Esther ordered a pink lady, which strikes me as a horrible drink at any time, but practically unbelievable before lunch. Still, I have never been a subscriber to the theory that you can tell something or other about a girl by what she drinks. About all I have ever been able to tell is whether she is a teetotaler or not.

I told the waiter to bring me three cans of beer, unopened, with an opener. He nodded as unconcernedly as though that were a usual order. I don't know myself why I had him bring the three at once, except that if you are going to be eccentric you might as well go the whole way. The memory of Charley sliding off that stool was fresh in my mind. It is pretty hard to do anything to an unopened can of beer.

Esther looked at me oddly. "Just a habit," I told her. "No sense in it here, but I got sick once on bar liquor."

She didn't make a point of it. I told her she was beautiful, which apparently made the right impression and took her mind off the beer, if she had been giving it much thought. The waiter served her drink and gravely set three cans of Budweiser before me, with a glass and a metal opener. I noticed that the bartender had come down to our end of the bar and was looking at me with frank curiosity, which made me feel a little better about the place. In his position I would have wanted a look at that crazy customer too. With some thought of improving my social standing, I ordered a couple of dollar cigars.

"I was a little nervous about asking you to come out with me," I told Esther.

Naturally she wanted to know why. I said that at first she hadn't been exactly cordial to the Colonel or me.

She made a gesture of distaste. "I wasn't cordial to him," she said. "You didn't give me much chance to be anything."

Show me a guy who doesn't eat up that kind of talk. I told myself she was a pretty nice girl, and very intelligent. We chatted for a time about nothing much.

When her drink was gone, she refused another. She excused herself, and suggested that I order lunch while she was gone. I reached across the table and grabbed her arm, forcing her back to the bench. She looked at me as though I were out of my mind, for which I didn't much blame her.

"It spoils a place for me if someone leaves the table," I told her. "If you really want to leave, we'll look up another place for lunch when you get back."

I watched to see how she would take it. The look of thunderstruck surprise was natural enough, and so, for that matter, was the stinging slap which I took from her other hand. It had certainly been a hell of a thing to say and do. When I released her arm, she walked rapidly back to the door marked "Ladies" without saying a word.

I looked around the room and saw that the waiter was politely ignoring the whole thing. The bartender, a husky, good-looking kid, appeared on the verge of vaulting over the bar. That could have been nothing more than chivalry.

She came back in a few minutes with her lips set and her eyes angry. "Please call me a cab," she told the waiter. She sat down at the booth, though.

I told her that my nerves were bad as a result of combat fatigue in the last war. I told her someone had tried to kill me last night. I told her sometimes I did things like that and was desperately sorry afterwards. I told her a lot more, and when her set expression softened a trifle, I motioned to the waiter and told him to cancel the cab. He bowed like a gentleman's gentleman and went to do it.

However, when I called for the check and suggested we go somewhere else to eat, she began to look mad again. I told her the bartender was a character named Lefty Louie whom I had once sent to jail, and I didn't want to hang around there.

When the waiter presented the check, he asked me politely if I wanted to take my remaining can of beer along. That was his only concession to human weakness during the entire incident.

Back in the car, things were a bit constrained. She pointedly suggested that I choose the next place, one that would be soothing to my nerves. I drove to one of the large downtown hotels, where we went into the bar.

Esther ordered another pink lady. I had a double Scotch, downed it quickly, and ordered a second. When that was down, my head was spinning faintly.

As a rule I am not a hard-drinking detective. I told Esther it felt good to be able to drink safely, without Louie around. After my third drink I suggested going into the dining room, and noticed that my voice was somewhat blurred. I had to watch my steps, too.

"I hope you don't think I'm drunk," I said.

"I hope you don't have any more," she answered. She wasn't exactly mad, but she wasn't as chummy as at the beginning of the afternoon. It was hard to blame her for that.

I told her that I was under a nervous tension because I had been working on a tough case. I told her that the police in this town were dummies who were going to be mightily surprised when I cracked it and made fools of them in the newspapers.

"Them and my smart partner," I said bitterly. "He thinks he can cut my throat in his reports and get all the credit. He's going to look like a damn fool when he sees what I turn up." I reached under the table and pinched her leg, which I would not have done without the third drink.

She got up from the table and stood looking at me with more contempt than anger showing.

"I guess I was wrong," she said. "I'll have to go now."

She walked out without looking back. Watching her go, I felt fairly sober, and a little sick of myself besides.

CHAPTER EIGHTEEN

BACK AT MY own hotel, Charley was inclined to be critical. "I thought you weren't to get out of my sight until tonight," he complained. "When I came out of that bar, you were gone."

"Something unexpected came up," I said morosely. I didn't care to talk about that afternoon.

The rest of the day wore along uneventfully, with Charley refiguring his expense account and me listening to the radio. We didn't talk much about the case until Thomas called. He told me that minute powder grains showed that Caldwell's hand had recently held a gun when it was fired. In his opinion that meant suicide, in spite of what he called my fancy theories. We quarreled a bit over the phone, just for the benefit of any switchboard operators who might be listening, and hung up.

At seven o'clock I told Charley he should be getting on with our plans for the evening, which precipitated another argument. He was inclined to be suspicious of my motives in giving him his assignment.

"I don't think it's necessary," he kept repeating.

I assured him that it was. I pointed out that next to hiring radio time, a date with Vera was the surest way of getting publicity around that hotel. I could think of no better method of letting all interested parties know that Charley was out for the evening and that I was alone. The fact that I had considerable curiosity as to how Charley would make out with Vera had nothing to do with the basic plan, although it may have influenced my advice to buy champagne for her.

He went along finally, still complaining, to have dinner in the restaurant downstairs and make his date with Vera. I phoned an order down to room service and ate a lonesome dinner which would have tasted better if I had had less doubts as to the evening's outcome.

When Charley came back at eight-thirty, he was quite pleased with himself. "She'll go," he announced. "I'm meeting her at ten o'clock. She seems like a nice friendly girl."

"She's all of that," I agreed. "Where are you going to take her?"

He looked faintly embarrassed. "She wants to go out to that roadhouse where they had the shooting last night."

"I should think you'd be ashamed to stick your head in the door. Besides, you're a celebrity there. Didn't you see your name in the paper?" I told him I had seen a headline in the evening paper which read: "Unidentified drunk carried out during the excitement." I added: "I'm going to clip it out and attach it to my final report on this case."

After that Charley wouldn't even talk to me until it was time for him to go down to meet Vera. Then he asked for the keys to the Ford. I objected that he would charge cab fare on his expense account anyhow, so he might as well take a cab. He just held out his hand, not considering that worthy of comment. I dropped the keys in it.

"Better leave me your extra gun," I suggested.

After a sharp look to be sure that I wasn't ribbing him about being a two-gun man, which I sometimes did, he dug it out of his suitcase and handed it to me. "Take care of yourself, kid," he said seriously. "I'd a lot rather be sticking around you." Ashamed of this emotional speech, he left immediately. I put the chain in place across the door.

After Charley was gone, I took off all my clothes but my shorts and, feeling a little silly, tried to tuck my own Mauser automatic in the waistband at the back. I was in a hurry, since the visit I was expecting might take place any time, and I could hardly bring myself to try out this scheme under Charley's critical eye. The idea was to make myself look unarmed beyond the shadow of a doubt. A glance at the full-view mirror in the bathroom showed that I looked all of that.

I took a couple of tentative steps and the Mauser slid down over my hips and fell to the floor, rapping my heel sharply as it landed. I was glad that experiment was secret.

Still, I was convinced that basically it was a good idea. I got a bathtowel and wrapped it tightly around my waist, knotting it at the side. That did the business. The Mauser stayed in place even when I made a couple of short leaps. I practiced a draw. It was reasonably fast, everything considered, but the blunt front sight scraped my back. I gave up the practice and sat down to wait.

Any wait of that sort is tedious, but this one understandably dragged out more than usual. Aside from a certain nervousness, which I didn't mind admitting to myself even though I didn't discuss it with the others, as to the purely physical hazards of this scheme, there was the additional danger of making myself look like a fool. And while I was reasonably confident of my basic premise, I was by no means sure that the killer would accept this carefully staged invitation to settle things that night.

At eleven-fifteen a knock came at the door. I waited until it was repeated, then took Charley's gun in my hand and walked to the door, opening it but leaving the chain on so that it could not swing wide enough to admit anyone.

"Who is it?" I asked.

"Hansen. Pete Hansen. I want to talk to you, Marks."

"Put both hands through the crack in the door," I told him. "I'm a little nervous about midnight visitors."

He laughed and did so. His voice sounded normal enough, and the laugh was a good-natured assent to an insane request. I opened the door.

He stared at me in understandable surprise. "Just going to take a bath," I explained. I waved him to a chair and tossed Charley's gun over on the sofa, well away from both of us. I seated myself on a corner of the desk. "Excuse the artillery, but I'm taking no chances. I've got a hunch I know how my boss was killed."

"What's that?" he asked. On close inspection he didn't look as calm as his voice sounded. The skin was tight about his eyes, and the fingers on his right hand drummed on the arm of his chair.

"I don't know who did it," I told him, "but I know how it was done. No one but me thought of the girl. When she's picked up, she is bound to break and tell us all about it."

I'll say this for him: he didn't fool around with a lot of conversation. He had made up his mind that he had to kill me, and he got on with it to the best of his ability. I could see from the way his jaw tensed that he was getting set to move, so when his hand dipped to his pocket I was ready.

He brought the gun out deliberately, having no cause to hurry since I was ten feet away from him with a chair between. The Mauser must have appeared to him to jump into my hand.

I had the split second necessary for careful aim. My shot caught him in the shoulder, solid enough to jar the gun out of his hand but not low enough to be lethal. I vaulted over the chair and rapped him on the head with the barrel of the Mauser before he could have known what hit him.

I flung open the door and fired twice more into the floor. It was tough on the carpet, but I wanted the noise in the hall. I took time then to grab a robe before running out into the hall. Esther Taylor was staring at me from the open door of her elevator. She took one look at the gun in my hand, and her stricken expression told me that my guess had been right.

"So," I said, "you were going to let him kill me just as he did the Colonel."

She moaned a little, not bothering to deny it. "Is he hurt?" She meant "dead" but could not bring herself to say it.

"He's gone either way," I told her brutally. "Murder packs a death sentence, you know."

My excuse, if I had any, was to shock her into a confession. It was too much, though. She wilted down in a dead faint.

CHAPTER NINETEEN

TONY AND I sat in the convertible at a point overlooking the sound. The day was not hot, but it was warm enough to be comfortable with the top down. The wide blue sweep of the bay below us, the snow caps of the mountains in the distance beyond the water, the quiet of the trees we were parked among, all combined to make it as pleasant a setting as could be found for an unpleasant scene I had been dreading. We hadn't talked on the drive from her home.

"It was nice of you to come," I said. "I know the sight of me doesn't bring up any agreeable associations. But I couldn't leave town without talking to you — telling you that I'm sorry for all that happened, and that I had to be any part of it."

She put her hand on mine for a minute. There wasn't any romance in the gesture, but it was friendly, conveying trust. "I want to talk to you, too, Jonny. I want to know everything that happened, and why. I think you'll tell it to me better than anyone else would."

Seeing my look of uncertainty, she added: "And you needn't leave out anything. Mother has explained about Dad not being my real father, and about the Colonel, and everything. She said I was sure to find out now. She doesn't like to talk about recent events, though, and she is really more confused than I am. You tell me, Jonny. I keep hoping it's not so bad as some of the things I have imagined. And nothing will change the way I feel about Dad."

Well, that much I could do for her. It probably wasn't as bad as the things that had been running through her mind. I was uncertain of her reaction to just one thing, and decided to clear that up first.

"Pete Hansen," I told her, "killed Thornton Caldwell."

She took it steadily. "That's horrible," she said after a minute, "but somehow not so bad as the thought of him committing suicide. It was the idea that he wanted to die that was so hard to bear."

So that was that. Hansen had meant nothing in particular to her — she was at least spared that much.

I started at the beginning, telling her how the Colonel had hired me from the agency to come here with him. "When he came," I said, "he had just located your family, after years of searching. He intended to blackmail Thornton Caldwell for a substantial part of his fortune. He remembered

Caldwell from the old days as a ruthless man, and he faced the fact that Caldwell might kill him. I was to be insurance that Caldwell didn't get away scot-free.

"When he saw the three of you together, saw that you were happy and well cared for and that both you and your mother loved Thornton Caldwell, he couldn't go through with it. Your own father wasn't such a bad sort, Tony. I liked him, was even fond of him, in the little time I knew him. You would have been too.

"He told Caldwell and your mother that he would go away without making trouble, and they believed him. He intended to do just that. If it hadn't been for Pete Hansen's crazy impulse none of this need have happened.

"Pete Hansen had not been present at all of the interview between your father and the Colonel. Your father trusted him a great deal, however, and told him something of what happened. He didn't tell him quite all — at least he didn't get across to Hansen his own conviction that the Colonel had changed his mind and was no further menace.

"Hansen went off the deep end. He had made a career of pleasing Thornton Caldwell, doing things Caldwell wanted done, priding himself on reading Caldwell's mind and doing those things even before Caldwell told him to. This time he went too far. He couldn't believe that your father really trusted the Colonel's intentions, and he himself couldn't believe that a man would give up such a clear opportunity for blackmail. He figured Caldwell would be happier and safer with the Colonel dead, so he killed him.

"That he was able to do it the way he did was just a lucky coincidence, or so it must have seemed to him at the time. The elevator girl, Esther Taylor, had been his mistress for several months. She was in love with him, and would do anything he said. She didn't know he intended murder when he killed the Colonel. He just asked her to take him up to the eighth floor and wait for him. He gained admittance readily, held his own gun on the Colonel until he disarmed him, then did the killing with the victim's own weapon.

"It only took a minute or so. When he got back to the elevator, he hurriedly told Esther what he had done, told her it would mean the electric chair for him if she didn't lie and say that no one came up in the elevator during the time in question.

"Later he decided that I was snooping around too much, and hired two of the Caldwell plant guards to kill me. He has charge of the guard force, and so could readily pick two men whose records would leave them open to that sort of a proposition.

"That was where his foot slipped, though. After the attack on me at the roadhouse, when Charley was put out of the way too, I knew the elevator girl must have some connection with the killer. Except for the two policemen, whom I was inclined to trust, she and the army corporal were the only people in town who had seen Charley and me together. They watched us in the hall together fooling with a door lock. The corporal just didn't fit as a suspect.

"Once it occurred to me to suspect her, the 'impossibility' of the Colonel's death being murder vanished. Assuming that she lied, the rest was easy. I took her out to lunch, let her see that I was suspicious of her, pretended to get drunk and let slip the fact that I hadn't taken anyone else into my confidence. I thought it would be a good bet that she would pass that on to her accomplice, whoever he or she was, and try to silence me that night as soon as it appeared that I would be alone. I got a lucky break, and it worked out."

We sat in silence for a few minutes. Then she asked: "And about Dad's death?"

"That occurred because Thornton Caldwell was a better man than Hansen gave him credit for being. Hansen told him about killing Colonel Smallwood immediately after it happened, and Caldwell was appalled. Still, he thought that Hansen had tried to help him, he could see nothing to be gained by exposing him, and he did nothing. Then when I brought you home that night and he learned that Hansen was carrying on with the killings, apparently intending to continue until anyone who might possibly suspect him was wiped out, Caldwell called a halt. He announced his intention of turning Hansen over to the police.

"Hansen admitted pulling Caldwell's own gun out of the desk drawer and shooting him. Then he placed the gun in Caldwell's hand and pulled the trigger again, so that there would be powder marks on the hand. He held the muzzle of the gun against a large book, which he carried away. After that he just removed one cartridge from the gun and took it away with him, leaving an almost perfect suicide behind.

"The thing which kept all of us from suspecting Hansen was his apparent lack of motive. He stood to lose much more by Caldwell's death than he could gain. It turned out that he had the best of all motives — self-preservation. If he hadn't killed Caldwell he would have stood trial for murder."

"Are you sure of all this, or just guessing?" she asked.

"Pretty sure. The girl was hysterical when she came out of her faint. She talked freely. We told Hansen the girl had confessed. He talked some more. None of it is very pretty."

Tony could follow my thoughts remarkably well. "You're feeling sorry for that girl, aren't you?"

I nodded. "Yes, I'm afraid so. She was just a dumb kid who was too crazy about a guy who was no good. If I had elected to play it another way, she would have gotten off fairly lightly for the first shooting — it could have been shown that she didn't know what was coming, and was no more than an accomplice after the fact. I tricked her into helping Hansen plot deliberately to kill me. A jury isn't apt to view her as quite so innocent now."

The silence lengthened again. She wasn't angry, but I felt that she had drawn herself away, and that she shared my own low opinion of my actions.

In an effort to lighten the atmosphere I gave her an expurgated account of my date with Vera. "Charley went out with her last night," I added. "It seemed the surest way of informing the world I would be alone to receive callers."

"How did he make out?" Tony asked.

"He refuses to discuss it," I said, "but he was putting cold compresses on a black eye this morning."

She was smiling again when I drove her home.

THE END

---

*Look for the next Bestseller Mystery, coming soon — "Lust for Vengeance"* (*formerly "Vengeance Street"*), *by Robert Bloomfield. "You'll find it hard to put down," says the New York Times.*

*FOR MYSTERY LOVERS* — The publishers of BESTSELLER MYSTERIES also publish the following paper-covered mystery books:

A MERCURY MYSTERY — The book now on sale is "THE PINBALL MURDERS," by Thomas B. Black. "Suspense, sex, and action," reports the Hartford *Courant*.

A JONATHAN PRESS MYSTERY — The book now on sale is "DIE LIKE A DOG" (formerly "The Hungry Dog"), by Frank Gruber. "Packed with action . . ." comments the *Saturday Review*.

All the mystery books published by MERCURY PUBLICATIONS are carefully chosen and edited for you by a staff of mystery experts. Sometimes they are cut to speed up the story, with the permission of the author or his publisher, but more often they are reprinted in full — complete and unabridged.

www.ingramcontent.com/pod-product-compliance
Lightning Source LLC
Chambersburg PA
CBHW020147180626
46810CB00004B/1780